Praise for

DOWN THE HUME

'Gritty and confronting, *Down the Hume* is a road map of life for a young man on a collision course with disaster.' – *Herald Sun*

'*Down the Hume* is an examination of the displacement experienced by those living on a city's fringes, lost in their own rapidly changing urban landscapes.' – *The Weekend Australian*

'This contemporary story is far more relevant and noteworthy than the nostalgic bush narratives that are considered the epitome of Australian storytelling.' – *Good Reading*

'To read *Down the Hume*, Peter Polites' fierce first novel, is to step into the literary wilds.' – *Sydney Morning Herald*

'Essential reading in these times of "border protection".' – *The Saturday Paper*

THE
PILLARS

ALSO BY PETER POLITES

Down the Hume

THE
PILLARS
PETER POLITES

hachette
AUSTRALIA

Lines from 'Thrush' by George Seferis, *Collected Poems*, courtesy of Princeton University Press.

hachette
AUSTRALIA

Published in Australia and New Zealand in 2019
by Hachette Australia
(an imprint of Hachette Australia Pty Limited)
Level 17, 207 Kent Street, Sydney NSW 2000
www.hachette.com.au

10 9 8 7 6 5 4 3 2 1

NATIONAL
LIBRARY
OF AUSTRALIA
A catalogue record for this
book is available from the
National Library of Australia

ISBN: 978 0 7336 4018 6 (paperback)

Cover design by Design by Committee
Cover photographs courtesy of Shutterstock
Author photograph courtesy of Stelios Papadakis
Text design by Bookhouse, Sydney
Typeset in 13.2/19.8 pt Adobe Garamond Premier Pro by Bookhouse, Sydney
Printed and bound in Great Britain by Clays Ltd, Elcograf S.p.A.

MIX
Paper from
responsible sources
FSC® C001695
www.fsc.org
The paper this book is printed on is certified against the
Forest Stewardship Council® Standards. McPherson's Printing
Group holds FSC® chain of custody certification SA-COC-005379.
FSC® promotes environmentally responsible, socially beneficial
and economically viable management of the world's forests.

I don't know much about houses
I know they have their own nature, nothing else.

George Seferis, 'Thrush'

1.

Rainbow flags will always trump the emerald green!

Kane paced from the sink to the table and kept mouthing off, his words running together.

A mosque? Down the road from here? No way!

Northern sun pushed through the glass doors that led to the backyard. Outside, Frenchie the French bulldog ran in circles, digging holes in the turf and lying in them. In the kitchen, only me and the stainless-steel appliances heard Kane's blowback. A slow cooker making osso bucco gurgled, tomatoes and flesh. A NutriBullet sat waiting for the morning green shake-a-thon. Neither device responded; instead a curra-wong warbled at exactly the moment when Kane chucked the local newspaper on the bench. The paper was open to the development section, showing graphs and a picture of the mayor. A heading of large black lettering: NOTICE OF APPLIC-ATION TO BUILD PLACE OF WORSHIP. Kane tapped one finger on the notice.

Kane's idea of a joke was to remind me that I was his tenant. He told me not to call him my housemate. Pano – he would say my name with that Australian accent, drawing out the vowels and reminding me that even though I had my proper Hellenic designation, it was never to be pronounced right. Pano . . . I am your landlord, he said, pausing and then adding a JK every time, but I never laughed. I responded with self-deprecating banter. I am a serf making humble pie with two birds from the bush, I said, and he didn't get the JK that I made.

As I read the proposal for an Albanian mosque, I heard Kane's voice say, It would be fine if it was a synagogue. Then – at least – the house prices would go up.

My fingers slipped a Ristretto coffee pod into the Nespresso machine and pushed the button. A string of coffee oil that looked like the tail of a rat fell into the Bodum double-wall thermo glass.

Kane pressed his buttocks against the kitchen island. A tribal tattoo in black ink ran over half his body; the spirals began under his left arm and went all the way down the side of his torso. They disappeared under his Y-fronts and emerged to cover his thigh. He'd got himself inked in Bali during a

Sydney Mardi Gras recovery session. In Bali, gay men getting tribal tattoos are as common as Nordic lesbians drinking Bintangs on the beach. But this ritual also represents a whimsical rite of passage, often initiated in the throes of an MDMA come down.

The black markings of indeterminate ethnic origin made him the most menacing-looking freelance IT consultant I'd ever met. As he talked, he crossed his arms over his chest and put one leg up on a stool. His affected pose made him look like he belonged on a gay influencer's Instagram page. All he needed was the buttless underwear. I curled my hands around the thermo glass and pulled it close to my chest. The scent of bay leaves emanated from the osso bucco in the slow cooker and Kane told me that he was working from home today.

I tried to look him in the eye and avoid examining his parts, and asked what he was going to do about the mosque. Kane dropped to the floor and started doing his daily Hindu push-ups and said that he wasn't keen on foreign things. From a plank position, he breathed in as he lowered himself down. On the exhale, he pushed forwards and arched his spine to look up at the ceiling. He told me he was going to start a residents' action group to prevent all this redevelopment of Pemulwuy. Kane was determined to keep the original character of a suburb that was built a whole ten years ago.

Pemulwuy is a suburb that pretends to be a gated community, without a gate. The people carry themselves with the air of pioneers. Once upon a time it was a brickworks that supplied the seventies suburban housing boom. Western Sydney grew and grew, the brickworks providing cheap materials to Parramatta, Merrylands and Liverpool. The bricks fortified three-bedroom houses and blocks of flats. Brick veneer and double brick veneer. Blond bricks for walls, earthen red bricks for fences with buttresses. When the sand ran low, the area was turned residential. It was named after an Aboriginal warrior who fought against the colonisers during the Frontier Wars. A reminder of Australia's history. But really the place was a big fuck you to all those suitcase-story migrants and working-poor blacks in the surrounding suburbs. Sleepy, anonymous and sterile, as calm as the man-made lake in its centre, Pemulwuy was designed not to offend and to be completely efficient. When it rained, the slight mound in the middle of the roads channelled the water to the gutters. Unlike the suburbs around it, Pemulwuy never had blocked drains and pooling rainwater.

Kane's motto = No Change. The oh-so-delicate property values in our street could go the wrong way. His morning jogs in all-black New Balance activewear among the McMansions would not be spent avoiding illegally parked cars. His afternoon walks with Frenchie the French bulldog in a rainbow harness would not involve the sight of suss crescent moons. Kosovan war trauma was trying to snake its way among the water features and kit homes. With Kane it wouldn't find a way in.

2.

Before Mum's brain became a beanbag, she taught me that the threat of a battle or a slight tremor in the economy could make society crumble. She prophesised that one day, while we all waited in line for skim caramel lattes, the stock markets would take a dip and hydrochloric acid would be flung in our faces.

She landed on Earth the exact day Hiroshima was blown up; her soul fell out of the *Enola Gay* at the same time the bomb did. Dealing with the after-effects of World War II created resilience and taught her life skills such as how to forage for wild greens and have knife fights with neighbours for food. It makes me sad to think that these are skills that the gen X and millennial snowflakes have lost.

On the days Mum gave me lessons on how to survive an apocalypse she sipped homemade raki. Raki is a Greek moonshine spirit that is only drunk with food; it comes in olive oil bottles and is also used to power tractors. She would pour seventy millilitres at a time into a coffee cup and tell me about seeing dead bodies. An uncle murdered by the invading German army, or her older brother who was killed by the Junta – even though these things happened decades apart. She would process the memories, take them out of the freezer of her mind, and two bodies appeared next to us in the kitchen. A swarthy uncle slit ear to ear on the speckled linoleum. A water-bloated brother leaning up against a cushioned chair. Mum getting progressively drunker on a spirit that was distilled in the backyard of one of the local unemployed Greeks.

Don't worry about the fact that you will never be able to afford a home. Worry about the economy shredding! That's when they will all come, with their black shirts and bayonets, and then you will see the drowned bodies and slit necks. And I would stand there and say, But Mum, why are you telling me this when I'm ten years old?

And with this fear in mind, like some Sarah Connor Clytemnestra, she taught me a number of post-apocalyptic life skills. The skillset was very specific to a post–World War II communist Greek village. In the garden just in front of the entrance to the apartment, she taught me how to grow tomatoes. She showed me how to use the white ash of an extinguished fire to wash my clothes in running water. A clear running stream was hard to find in the concrete wastelands of the suburbs. The closest thing was the Cooks River, which had running water but also had more metals than a mine. A river so polluted from illegal dumping that white, mutated fish with three eyes would leap out of it. So these lessons had to wait for heavy rainfall; when the gutters overflowed they became our creeks. She led me down to the street in full view of the neighbourhood bullies, took my skid-marked Y-front jocks, and wet them with gutter water. Then she got ash that she had prepared in a fire bin on our balcony and rubbed the ash on the skid marks.

In this Acropolis apocalypse, fermenting wine in a laundry sink was another handy skill that I learned. Wine could be traded for other goods, if the systems of finance collapsed. Along the way Mum picked up other tips, too. From Indian co-workers she learned about the healing powers of turmeric on inflamed body parts. From Korean neighbours she learned how succulents such as cactus and aloe vera could be transformed into beauty products to increase luminosity of skin, glossiness of hair and overall attractiveness. This would be useful if I ever needed to use my flora-enhanced good looks as a currency. Knowing the limitations of my general skills and abilities, Mum assumed that I would need to do sex things in Apocalyptoville to survive.

3.

When I left my room after my morning procrastination Kane intercepted me in the hallway and asked what I was doing. He stood in the doorway of the home office. Behind him the printer whirred like a six-barrel rotary machine gun. I looked at the carpet and told him that I was taking a constitutional, going for a wander and heading over to Bankstown to meet an old high school friend called Basil. The noise of the printer filled the pauses in our dialogue. Kane put one hand up on the doorframe and leaned towards me. He said that I couldn't be going for a wander and a constitutional as they were two very different things. He pressed his finger into my chest to make his point. He said that one signified purposeful vigour and the other implied an empty-headed leisurely stroll.

Kane suggested that as I take my constitutional I put flyers into letterboxes. Initially I said no, telling him that I was looking for inspiration to complete my second book of prose poems and that I had a casual form of anxious jitters about meeting my old acquaintance.

Kane popped out of the doorway, interested in my meeting. He asked what Basil did, but he really wanted to know if Basil was hot. I said to Kane that he was a scorching property developer with soccer-star thighs. A real jock fucker with a winner attitude too. When we were teenagers I used to hide behind the school gym and watch him lying on a bench doing an incline press. He attempted to rock a stringlet but had no definition. Still was hot though.

Once Kane's jealousy peaked, I let him down. Basil was straight.

With one hand on my upper arm and one hand holding the flyers, Kane stepped closer to me. He craned his neck to look closer at me. As he held my arm, he started stroking his thumb up and down, kneading my tricep muscle. Kane asked me again if I would distribute the flyers for him. You could just put them in letterboxes as you walked out of the suburb? Each syllable emphasised by the stroke of the thumb.

A year earlier, I had discovered Kane of Pemulwuy on a website called A Queer in Both Your Houses – the premier website connecting gay and lesbian flatmates. For our first meeting, I wore plain chinos and a checked shirt. I sat opposite him on the couch while he interviewed me. There were no decorative cushions interrupting the clean leather lines of the modular sofa, and I saw this as a good sign that he prioritised an efficient aesthetic in his furnishings. I pointed to the replica Noguchi coffee table and asked if he liked modernist sculpture. He answered by telling me that he was thinking about putting modern sculptures in the backyard, and I realised he didn't know what a Noguchi coffee table was. I didn't correct him. If I had explained that I had a deep understanding of modernism and the Bauhaus, my knowledge of post-World War II design trends would have made me appear pretentious and exposed me. But the cloak of normality I was trying to convey was destroyed when I told him that I wrote, and that I was currently living on a government grant. When I told him I wrote poems his face wrinkled. He asked, Does anyone even read them? I said no; I know poets who have sold fewer books than they have Twitter followers. He laughed. I had taken myself down a peg and smoothed everything out. It was that ole Australian self-deprecation, a familiar signifier that I was no tall poppy. He called later that day to ask me to move in with him.

It was the house and the suburb that sparked my aspirations. There were no old couches on the street, there were no cars in front yards on cinder blocks and no high-density apartments. When I arrived home I could see how far I was from Mum's messy apartment crammed with papers and broken

TVs; from share houses with funky junkies and neglected pets. Finally, I had found a place where I could sit down and drink a tall glass of iced mineral water, garnished with cucumber.

On the day I moved in with Kane, I noticed the framed rainbow flag hanging in the hallway and my arms shuddered uncontrollably. Perhaps it was the elemental magic the six colours held, more likely it was because I had been lifting heavy boxes all day. Kane had purchased the flag in Rome. On the ugly rock-filled beaches of the Mediterranean he had used it to dry the salt water and Mykonos cum off his body. Its edges were frayed, the colours muted; sunrays and salt had faded it. On arriving back in Australia he'd had it dry-cleaned and custom-framed. Looking closer at the yellow stripe, I saw a faint stain that could have been the industrial-strength Euro jizz of an olive picker.

By the powers vested in him by the rainbow flag, Kane pushed the flyers into my hands. They were printed on pink paper and the Australian flag looked very gay: it could have been on a fag rag's masthead. The flyer included a scanned reproduction of the mosque development notice, surrounded by warnings of property price drops in our neighbourhood. There were arrows pointing down towards a dollar sign. His mobile phone number was printed on the bottom. Exasperated with Kane and his relentless rainbow, I said yes, yes, yes, I would deliver some of the flyers and then make my way to Bankstown. As I exited the front door, Kane yelled out to me, reminding me to tell people that refreshments would be available. Refreshments! he yelled. Tell people about the refreshments!

I walked down the empty streets of Pemulwuy towards the lake. It was a Wednesday and the cars had already done their morning bottleneck out of the suburb. Where the houses didn't have freestanding letterboxes, I had to go up to the doors and put the flyers in the metallic slots. From backyards dogs barked, in front yards cats tried to be my friend. The birds watched from above as though I was Tippi Hedren and they were hoping I might trip.

A young mother passed me in the street. She pushed a pram and held a carnation in her hand. Her shirt was made of a wicking fabric that ate sweat. The orange colour of her fake tan stopped at her neck, so her jawline and face were a slightly different colour. I couldn't see inside the pram – she might have been pushing her child, a doll or a chihuahua. Her voice squeaked as she asked me about the flyers. I explained about the mosque and she started her sentence with a You Know What? She didn't have a problem with Muslims coming into the neighbourhood and indeed her friends were 'some of the good ones'.

I told her that my flatmate was my landlord and I was just a serf. She introduced herself to me as Lorna, pronouncing it like she was going to a job interview. I told her that he was really worried about house prices dropping, which could have a ripple effect across the broader Sydney housing market, causing the bubble to pop and heralding an acid-in-the-face-flinging apocalypse. She played with the carnation in her hand and said with the efficiency of a human resources mediator: I see we have an unresolvable issue here. I nodded my head in agreement, and said that it might lead to a Mexican stand-off in an Australian suburb named after an Indigenous freedom fighter. Both parties cannot be satisfied.

When Lorna talked, I picked up that she code switched. You know what? she said in a Western Sydney accent. But when she summarised the mosque problem, her tone sounded corporate, like someone reading the Threats part of a SWOT plan.

She leaned over the pram and fiddled with whatever was inside. She pulled a blanket over the child, doll or chihuahua. I heard something yap from inside. Lorna said, I mean, gee, it would be fine if it was a synagogue – then the prices would go up. She would leave the baby with its father to attend the meeting and discuss the problem. I told her that I would make some refreshments available.

Walking through the tundra-scape of suburbia, many of the garages were open, waiting for cars to return. Front gardens were done in a Palm Springs-style; they had bulbous succulents rising out of smooth rocks. I walked up the pebbled path of a single-storey house with a garage taking up fifty per cent of its frontage, and put a flyer in the door slit. Leaving, I noticed an aloe vera plant, its leaves pointing in every direction. I heard my mum talking about homemade beauty products and reflected on the hand of the Doomsday Clock being a few minutes from midnight, and I swooped on the plant and plucked the biggest stem. It made a loud snap, and then I heard the catches of two locks release. There was an attention-seeking cough and a man said, Excuse me.

I spun around to see a bearded middle-aged man standing in the doorway. He wore chinos and a blue-and-white Ralph Lauren polo shirt with the collar popped; it had a galaxy of pills on it from being washed and dried haphazardly. In case I had been in any doubt that the man was wearing Ralph Lauren, the polo logo covered most of his chest. I wondered if he had ever ridden a horse and held a mallet at the same time.

The man asked if I was stealing his plant as I stood there holding the frond in my hand. I used the classic smoke-and-mirrors technique to get out of the situation, the smoke being my words and the mirrors my wild gestures. My hands stirred the air as I talked, waving around the aloe leaf and pointing out the vacant lot where the proposed mosque would be. There! Over there! I said, conducting a one-way conversation with my polo-wearing friend. As I walked back to give him another flyer, I saw past him into the house. On the wall facing the door was a picture of the Kaaba hung above a rococo side table. The table had curved gilded legs and a marble top. On it were keys with a green key chain and a charging station for smartphones. The man introduced himself as Wahid, and when I squinted suspiciously at him, he reintroduced himself as Wally.

You must be worried about house prices going down, I said.

He held the flyer in his hand and shook it once, as if to make the lettering go into focus. His knuckles reached up to his face; they had thick black hair all over them. He slowly scratched his chin. Among the sound of rustling, tiny flakes of beard dust fell onto the pink flyer. He said that it would have been fine if it was a synagogue, then at least the house prices would go up. When Wally said this it sounded anti-Semitic, as if Jewish people had a suspicious amount of wealth. I scanned his black beard and large nose for signs of someone who would support the mass incarceration of Jewish people. He had a beard, but it tended to the fashionable rather than the religious. In spite of the picture of the Kaaba he had a Ralph Lauren shirt with a giant logo. His fancy table and on-trend beard told me that he would come to the meeting. There would never be solidarity before the market.

I pointed to the phone number on the flyer and invited him to call Kane. To make it more enticing, I told him that there would be refreshments available, such as cucumber sandwiches cut into quarters. Two brown eyes up-downed me, and he scratched his black beard again. I informed him that there would also be halal samosas and we both nodded at each other. I started stepping backwards, waving bye and saying bye. The door inched closed, Wally telling me that he would see me soon, repeating thank-you and making our cheeks flush red.

I walked out into the middle of the empty street. Only five metres across, it was a stretch to call this a road. I had often seen two cars approaching from opposite directions and one of them have to pull over so the other could pass. Either side of where I stood, the houses were fresh. The recently laid front lawns looked like upholstery instead of grass. I walked in the middle of the empty roads to the bus stop.

Over the year I had lived here, I had seen plots of land sold and houses built up from nothing. I had seen the different kinds of workmen who assembled the frames, laid the bricks and rendered the walls. The houses were emerging from the inside out, nests of dreams, built to a plan.

4.

Bankstown was a reminder of my teenage failures. When I got there, I took a tour of the old shops in Saigon Place. The place had changed in subtle ways – it was cleaner now and the tables of fruit and perspex signs radiated primary colours. And there were fewer junkies around. But vendors still sold green pandan waffles and the bunch of old men still met on the corner to gamble for money. Amid the newer Viet supermarkets and accountants' offices stood the Olympic Continental Delicatessen. The deli had been around for as long as anyone could remember, serving the Greeks and making its own salami and bratwurst. I walked in and stocked up on the essentials: mastic, ION almond chocolate and halva from Thessaloniki.

I stopped at the window of Vas Bros Real Estate and looked at all the apartments for sale, trying to find the logic in a two-bedroom apartment in Bankstown selling for half a million dollars. There were professional photos of men in polyester suits holding gavels and standing outside houses. A human-sized decal of a balding man in his finest suit with a dental-work smile grinned at me like I wasn't in on the joke.

As I stood examining the grids of houses, two hands slid across my face and blocked my vision. A pulse flickered up my spine and I dropped the shopping bags. I put my own hands over the pair covering my face and said, Um, new phone who dis? I cupped my fingers around the hands and tried to shift them down.

Lips touched my ear lobe, and a voice whispered, We don't want faggots looking at property around here.

A hot blast of air scraped into my eardrum. I took a deep breath in and reached behind me, feeling for the person's crotch. My fingers found a belt and I undid the metal loop, right there on the main road with cars passing and the tread of heels. When the belt flipped open, I moved my hands expertly to the zipper of the pants. The hands came away from my face, my sight was restored, and I turned around.

Basil stood before me wearing the tightest pinstripe pants and a checked pink shirt with a shiny tie that reflected the sun. He snorted and then wiped his nose with his finger. Fuck, Pano, you're still a high school faggot.

There were sweat marks under his arms going almost down to his waist. I told him I was sorry I never called him back after high school for hangs. I meant to, but then I discovered how good ecstasy and gay nightclubs were, and I couldn't open my Ericsson clamshell.

I picked up my shopping bags and we walked into the cafe next to Vas Bros Real Estate. We sat down at a table and I asked him about post-high-school life. He said that he had expanded the construction company that his dad, Spiro, retired from. He was involved in buildings all around the west. He called himself a great man, another empire maker, like his dad or Alexander the Great.

While he was talking he waved to the barista girl with a messy ponytail who knew him by name. As he raised his arm, his bicep strained the material of his shirt. When she came over, Basil gave her one hundred per cent of his attention and in a caramel-sleaze voice said he would love a bit of her macchiato, then gave a wink. She sighed, and I asked for a long black.

We sat on upside-down crates and the small table had just enough room for our elbows. Basil's face up close was as sculpted as his body. The thick, shaped curve of his eyebrows made him look constantly surprised. His face was polished marble offset all the way to his hooked nose.

Basil told me about his girlfriend, Kamilla. He specified that her name was spelled with a K, turning the letter into a syllable, *kaay*. They had just moved in together.

In high school Basil had indiscriminate tastes, like most teenage boys. He had a thing for girls who wore chokers and baby-doll dresses, the alterna-Anglo girl of the late nineties. He also dated girls with honey-blonde hair and hard bodies from netball. I knew he had brief couplings with Greek and Leb girls, but he claimed the thick coats of foundation and matte-red lips turned him off: Nah. Too much makeup. No good!

Some of them were just as good at soccer as he was, and I suspected that this was the real reason. Basil was too precious to date a winger that could dribble a ball around him.

I remembered a moment in the playground when I looked at Basil's smooth, muscled legs in shorts. There were droplets of sweat running down them like tears and his crying legs made me ache.

He was one of the first boys in our school to have the hair waxed from his legs, claiming all athletes did it. Later, he was a trailblazer for the young male wogs by using an experimental new laser treatment to remove all his body hair. In our last year of high school, I overheard him talking about how important natural beauty was to him, which was why he didn't bang wog girls, because they spent too much time on themselves.

Barista Girl put two coffees in front of us. Basil called her love and then sweetie. A grimace flashed across her face before she forced a smile. He pulled out his phone to show me a picture of Kamilla and him at the beach, sitting on the sand together. Basil wore Carrera aviator sunglasses and his collarbones were red. She had buttress cheekbones and injectable-plump lips, and her white string bikini top stood out against her orange skin. Her collarbones were freckled and her long black hair looked dyed. She had a wide space between her breasts. I told Basil that she looked nice and Basil told me that he was finally into ethnic-looking chicks.

While I sipped on coffee Basil asked what I'd been doing for the past few years. I told him I had written a book, but I didn't tell him that it was published by a small press and only three hundred copies had been sold. He cocked his head and licked his lips and said that I should write a book about him.

I had to resist the urge to roll my eyes. When I introduced myself as a writer, depending on the individual's degree of narcissism they might say, Do I have a story for you!

In a world where headphones create a soundtrack to the film each individual is starring in, feelings about everyday events are often mistaken for something unique.

I maintained my silence. He said that he was planning to make a run at local council, and the fact that an author was writing a biography would be a wonderful human-interest story for the local rags, plus the book would be a record for his children and grandchildren. I fingered the rim of my coffee cup and said I would have to think about it. He told me an amount. It was a throwaway sum for him, but would be enough to cover my rent for a while. I ummed and said that I thought his story had real potential, even movie-like qualities. The world needed his unique experiences.

Ka-ching.

5.

On one side of a blue-and-gold Jonathan Adler Versailles-style serving platter I arranged quartered cucumber sandwiches with the points upwards. On the other side of the platter were baked halal samosas for Wally. I put the culturally appropriate platter on the table and arranged tall green bottles of mineral water around it.

I made catering suggestions for the meeting, keen to show Kane I could host. Perhaps nuts and seeds in bowls, next to haloumi and feta with slices of Greek sourdough. But Kane's tastes extended only to the range of foods that he grew up with. My ideas were too out there. When he said the words 'too out there', I no longer tried to advocate my people's cuisine. As a serf in the house, I deferred to the landowner.

When you look up to someone, you must tilt your head. And when you tilt your head, you become smaller than them. It's easy to mistake height for power. It's also easy to mistake money for strength.

Lorna was the first guest to arrive. As I was wiping a few crumbs off the edge of the platter, the doorbell chimed, and Kane opened the door. Before Lorna stepped into the house, she looked down the hallway and saw me standing in the kitchen. Her hair was freshly straightened and she wore a cold-shoulder fuchsia blouse made from a shiny material. The blouse draped over her body, showing her décolletage, collarbones as refined as an alloy. She wore selvedge denim jeans in a loose boyfriend style with gold stitching. On her feet were Adidas Originals three stripes. Her look could be called suburban exceptionalism – an outfit suitable for a trip to the supermarket or enjoying a glass of moscato at book club.

She noticed the framed rainbow flag hanging just inside the doorway. I watched her mouth change shape as she tried to make sense of the house and our relationship. Kane ushered her through the house, Lorna stepping delicately on the carpet and glancing discreetly at the objects around her. She pulled out a chair at the head of the dinner table and sat down. I thought it was presumptuous of her to take the leadership seat. She poured herself mineral water and politely picked up one of the sandwiches. Holding the quarter between her fingers, she took a quick, careful look to see what was inside.

Kane sat next to Lorna; we began social lubrication by talking about the weather. Weather weird? Yes! Yes! It's weird for this time of year. How much weather are we having? I prefer the old weather! Yes! Yes! The old weather was a weather of sorts.

I interrupted the socialising by flicking a finger at Lorna and saying that I was surprised that someone with her skin tone could pull off a fuchsia cold-shoulder blouse. Lorna exhaled and took a gulp of water. She told us that her mind had the fog of new motherhood. No one ever tells you how happy you will be! And no one – ever – tells you how completely you lose yourself to the lump of flesh that is a baby!

A guilty part of her missed the scheduled nine-to-late-night corporate life. The blouse was from her old life, and she wore it to remind herself of her pre-baby self. She told us that she had come to this residents' action group against the mosque to keep her knives sharpened.

There was a knock on the door. Kane left and came back into the kitchen with Wally. He wore a red polo shirt and aqua chinos; this time the horse mallet man was a tiny bit more discreet. As he walked into the kitchen he asked which country the flag in the hallway belonged to. The room filled with silence; smirks appeared on lips. Kane coughed. I told Wally that it was from one of those Scandinavian countries in Northern Europe. Wally praised the flag's brightness and I mentioned how much I liked the clean lines of Scandi furniture.

At the meeting the four of us decided that religion was never the problem. This wasn't a problem with Islam, rather that a religious building might lower the property values. We noted that Wally would make a great figurehead for the campaign. This would prevent any accusations of Islamophobia. I found an ivory-white plate and put two samosas on it. I suggested to Wally that he was hesitant about our opposition to the mosque. He agreed. He thought his parents would never accept his opposition to a mosque, even if it wasn't his own denomination. Lorna readjusted the puzzle pieces in her head. She rubbed her temples with her fingers, poured more mineral water into her glass and drank. Her lips became moist rose gold. Her movements were elegant but when she communicated directly she became a slick Doberman. She had a direct-to-face stare and a sleek chest.

She looked Wally square in the eye: It's not that you don't want an Albanian mosque to be built. You don't want anything that could lower your house prices and affect your wealth and your children's future.

Wally looked as confused as I was, but Lorna continued, Just think about the values, the VALUES. Just think about how the values will go down. Imagine what your family will think if you hadn't done everything in your power to protect your money and your children's future!

Wally's nods became larger. He seemed pleased with this explanation.

Kane suggested a series of press releases and photos for the local paper. Wally posing with his young family on the front lawn, perhaps holding the Qur'an while his wife stood next to him wearing a sari that was subtle enough to say middle class but exotic enough to say legitimate foreigner. The campaign needed to read as local community opposition to changes in the neighbourhood. The subtext would be 'new Australians say no to mosque'.

Lorna came at us with her pre-mum life of PR experience. Listening to her, I realised how lazy my judgements were. My initial thoughts required revisiting; I had thought she was stupid. Now I realised she had a sparkly personality and the perfect degree of aggressiveness for someone working in public relations. Most recently, she had worked as communications manager for a major rugby league club called the Deities. Theirs were the highest-paid footballers in the league and the club was often in breach of the salary cap. The Deities were the heart of Western Sydney, its real mascots, godlike and always in the news for sexual assaults, cocaine bust-ups and forcing abortions on the model girlfriends they met through social media. Lorna's job was to train them to talk to the camera. It sounded great to treat a muscle jock as though he was Eliza Doolittle. The most effective technique she had found with those men was telling them to pretend that they were apologising to their mum.

Our conversation became a spiral; we circled over ideas and points we could go forward on together. The campaign began to take shape. Kane's back straightened. My elbows fell off the table, while Lorna held a glass in both hands close to her chest, her eyes alive. Wally was the first to leave, citing work in the morning. Lorna asked to switch the mineral water for merlot.

As Kane and Lorna drank, I wrote down a series of actions that needed to be taken. I handed the piece of paper to Lorna and her eyes scanned it. She opened the calendar on her phone and input the information. I left the two of them at the table, sipping wine.

6.

Basil drove me around Bankstown in his Mustang and showed me all the buildings, properties and empty lots that he had his fingers in: That one I'm acquiring. That empty lot will become a car park. That's gonna be apartments.

The driver's seat was angled at almost forty-five degrees and he leaned back while holding one hand on the steering wheel. On his wrist was a watch with a thick golden band and a large face encircled by diamonds. The windows of the car were tinted, but I could see outside perfectly. When we rolled to a stop at traffic lights, I looked dead on at people knowing that they couldn't see inside the car.

It was my first time in what Western Sydney residents called a 'luxury vehicle'. It wasn't the Mustang's heated leather seats that impressed me. It wasn't the silver horse running across the steering wheel or the sporty gearstick. It was the way the cabin of the car protected and separated you from the outside world. It glided over the road, low to the ground, and we couldn't hear the rumble of trucks or the beeping of aggressive drivers. It made driver and passenger feel an immediate intimacy.

We pulled up at an intersection, and Basil pointed to a residential tower. Can tell ya the history 'bout that place! Once I got the permits – bam! He hit the steering wheel. The building was seven storeys tall. His chest puffed out as he told me the name he picked for the tower – Apex Point. It was above the entrance in a serif font. The northeast-facing balconies were shielded from the sun by a metal awning. The balconies on the other side had glass barriers and looked over the main road. The concrete render on the walls was already stained with water damage; it made the building look as if it was decomposing.

Basil hit the steering wheel – bam! – his palm connecting to the silver horse, every time he wanted to emphasise a point. At first it shocked me, then I could predict when it was going to happen. His monologue filled up the cabin around me; there was no place to go but to listen. I was entranced by the way he used words to put people under his control. Away from where he could see, I ran my knuckles against the leather seat that I was sitting on. Up and down the leather seat on my side. I could feel the smooth black skin on my fingers and I pretended it was his body.

We pulled up next to a newly built nine-storey apartment block. The building's walls were painted a light grey and the balconies were white. A four-storey-high superfluous scalene triangle was attached to the balconies on one side. Basil called it a design feature, said it made the building a statement piece. This building was called The Endeavour. Basil said that his favourite part of development was naming places. I asked him how he came up with the name and he threw his hand up in the air. Yeah, well . . . see that triangle there? It's like a sail, n' when I saw it, I guess . . . I wanted to remind people of boats – boats, you know.

The air conditioning in the car was on full blast, cold air running across my nose. Basil told me a story about The Endeavour. He leaned over and put his hand on the back of my neck. He looked into my eyes and pulled me towards him. Too close, almost close enough to kiss. Off the record, yeah-yeah, okay? he said to me. We submitted the plans with only eight storeys. Eight storeys flat. Bam. Because – you know – Bankstown fucking airport, fucking tiny planes flying all over the joint, buildings can't get too tall. But then when we built that place, that place right there, made it nine storeys. Decided to cop a fine instead. The fine? Nothing, bro! Only one-sixth of what an apartment in the building costs. Peanuts.

He broke his grip on my neck. I leaned back in my seat and turned to look outside as he drove us out of the suburb and to his father's house by the river.

We pulled into a driveway. The front yard was concreted over in a single-pour slab. A lemon tree and an olive tree grew out of the concrete. Each of the trees was surrounded by a circle of bricks; their roots had broken the concrete around them. A white concrete banister wrapped around the front veranda and down the stairs. In between two columns was a wooden rococo door, carved with swirls and panel of mass-produced stained glass in the middle. The red bricks of the house were rough as a rock and outlined with pure white mortar.

Basil beeped the horn and an old wog with a fisherman's cap came out. He wore blue canvas pants and a workman's jacket over a flannel shirt. Basil jumped out of the car to hug him, but his dad put his arms up to stop the gesture and then punched him on the shoulder. I was introduced as an author writing a book about Basil. The old man's chest puffed up, and he told me to call him Spiro. His lower eyelids hung loose. There were tiny red veins in the whites of his eyes and a layer of grey encroached around his brown irises.

He welcomed us into the house and I followed them down the hallway. I walked past a series of Greek icons, their wide eyes looking over me, their golden skin welcoming God's light. At the end of the hallway was a little table with a burning candle, fresh wattle stems and a photo of what must have been Basil's mum. The photo had been taken at a wog function. In front of her was a table covered in a white cloth, cutlery laid out. A smile was smeared across her face and her eyes were filled with light. I recognised Basil's broad hook nose on her. A pretty woman, high cheekbones, big eyes. A lot of the space in the photo was taken up by her permed hair. She wore a purple sequinned dress that covered her shoulders. The extreme colours of the eighties were painted on her face. Black eyeliner and blue eyeshadow. The rouge on her cheeks had an expressionist quality. Her lips were glossed with bright pink.

I stood in front of the shrine, looking at the picture. My hand reached for the wattle involuntarily; my fingertips brushed the flowers. Basil's father turned around and saw me. He came over to me and paused before moving my hand away. He told me that her favourite flowers were Australian. There was a moment of silence until I stopped looking at the picture and walked into the open-plan living area.

The living room had a tiled floor leading into the kitchen. A brown Chesterfield sofa and La-Z-Boy armchair faced a large flat screen television. I sat on the sofa and Spiro went to make us coffee. Basil said that he needed to make a phone call, and left the room. His father complained about that telephone his son was always on. He brought over the briki and two cups with saucers.

Spiro said he was proud of his son. But his son spent too much time on business. Not enough time on creating a family of his own.

Before he poured the coffee, the old man asked me if I wanted the kamaki – a gesture of goodwill, offering me the bubbly froth on top of the coffee.

I asked him how Basil started, and he gestured with his thumbs towards himself. Spiro had begun working in building when he came to Australia in the sixties. At first he laboured on sites around country towns, not welcome in the 'villages', as he called them. People spat in his face but his friends protected him from unfriendly locals. He dug holes and carried planks and bricks. Eventually he got a carpentry apprenticeship and made frames for houses. After ten years making frames he had enough experience and contacts to build his own houses. He passed on all the knowledge to his son. As he told me this he balled his fist and hit his own chest. I am a proud moit, he said.

I asked Spiro if he lived with anyone else; he clicked his tongue and raised his eyebrows, replying to me by doing the Mediterranean no.

Spiro told me a story from when he was coming up from his early days as a builder. He had a pet German shepherd who followed him everywhere. It would sit on the back of the ute when he travelled from site to site. He called it by his mother-in-law's name, Esther. Once Esther the German shepherd got oil paint on her coat and Spiro couldn't get it off. He got an old rag and removed the paint with turpentine. The dog's coat was cleaner than before, and he let her go dry in the sun. When he came back the dog had been licking her coat and had ingested the turps. Esther got sicker and sicker. Spiro gave the dog milk to try to mediate the toxicity. On the first day she began to go blind; by the third day she wasn't able to see him. He told me about taking her neck in his hands and killing her.

Spiro kept looking at his hands, and the room was silent until Basil came back, complaining about the phone reception. Fucking river! Fucking trees!

Basil's phone rang again. Spiro sighed so loudly that the room exhaled with him. Some people work to live, he said, others work to try and make the dead proud.

We left Spiro's house when he started yawning. When his son tried to tell him something, his eyelids crept slowly over his cataracts. He was an old man, and it was mid-afternoon, time for rest.

As Basil drove me back to my house, I told him that I would begin his book with his father's story.

7.

The annoying barks of Frenchie the French bulldog woke me. Kane must have gone to work and was not there to console the creature. I tried pulling the sheet over my head, but my feet kept pulling it down. Inside my room was a small double bed; my inbuilt wardrobe was half filled with books. On the desk was a yellow writing pad and my laptop.

A clean house empty of people is one of the great pleasures of life. It ranks up there with having only positive memories of your mother and forgetting the times she made you wash your undies in a gutter of rainwater to get ready for the Acropolis Apocalypse.

There were three loud knocks on the front door and then the doorbell rang. Frenchie the French bulldog intensified his barking. I got up and went to see who it was. Walking through the living area, I saw that Kane had left the local newspaper on the coffee table. It was open to a picture of Wally posing with his family. The headline read 'Local Muslims Opposed to Mosque'. The picture was taken in front of his house. Wally stared directly at the camera and his arms were folded; standing a distance behind him, his wife was holding one child in her arms and the other child by the hand. Wally's eyebrows looked bushier than I remembered. His mouth puckered on the precipice of an alpha-male grunt.

Three more knocks on the door, increasing in strength. When I opened it, Wally stood there. Heya, buddy, I said with a friendly punch on the shoulder. Look at you in the paper! I held it up.

Wally stood with his hands at his sides, tilted his head and started yelling at me. I took a step back, put my hands out and asked him to speak more clearly. He pointed at the newspaper in my hand and told me to read it.

I stood in the hallway and Wally stood at the door. Light filtered from behind him and fell onto the paper. The journalist was called Rebecca White, and this Becky White adhered to her name by adding salt and pepper to the article. She provided commentary: 'While I speak to Wahid, his wife stays in the background, tending silently to the children.' The wife was described in several places as quiet, silent and wordless. The article also quoted an unnamed terrorism expert who gave a potted history about the conflicts between the different sects of Islam. A local politician was given the last word: 'Australia is no place for old-world tribal tensions.'

When I'd finished reading the article, I looked up at Wally. His cheeks were puffing as he breathed in and out. He told me that he was meditating, and I asked him if he meant praying. We stood at the doorway and I sent an SMS to Kane saying we needed to come up with another game plan.

Frenchie came running up the hallway. He stood behind me and barked at Wally.

8.

The article about Wally that misrepresented him as sectarian was nothing new for the newspapers of this country. They twist, they beat up, they lie and sensationalise. If only I had remembered my personal relationship to the nation and the history this came from.

Just before Sydney's most recent white supremacist riots I was walking along the promenade of a beachside suburb licking a chocolate and lemon gelato when young men in a station wagon drove past me and yelled, Wog! Wog! Wog! I raised a clenched fist and shouted at them, How dare you! Wog is an acronym for Western Oriental Gentleman! But my response was lost among the clatter of the beer cans they threw at my head. One of the empty beer cans connected; the shock knocked me over. As my ass landed on the pavement, the chocolate and lemon gelato landed all over my matching summer wear and it made me reflect on the real origins of the word.

Wog is a term specific to outposts of the British Empire and dates to an era when reds were under the bed and the bedsheets were made from asbestos. At the time we still feared a yellow peril using chopsticks to cross the Timor Sea and invade our girt-by-sea lamington landmass with their hammers and sickles. Lucky for us we had our cricketing hero Allan Border dressed in whites as blinding as the sun. He spent decades standing sentry at the borders of Australia ready to whomp those silk pyjama wearers.

The word became prominently used around the early eighties, when it started to be reclaimed by the people it defined. It found its way into sketches on television featuring Greek stereotypical characters. One such character was Marika from *The Comedy Company*. My mother is not named Marika and she did not work in a fruit market. Marika was played by a white comedian named Mark Mitchell. He wore an apron, dark, curly wig and hammed it up with a tzatziki accent. When we watched Mark Mitchell play Marika the Mediterranean matriarch on the television we laughed at him and liked him because he was a man wearing a dress and his funny accent reminded us of ourselves. Later we learned to stop laughing at Mark Mitchell playing Marika because we should be the ones to remind ourselves of our funny accents. We still found men in dresses funny though.

I was never into dresses, I was into men. But if I were into dresses I would prefer short tailored numbers, with clean, military lines. Marika used to make jokes about having to shave her face, because Greek women are hirsute and a Greek woman in the shower was a Gorilla in the Mist. My mum never had more than one or two stray hairs on her face, thanks to a shoebox of tweezers in our bathroom.

By the time I was eight years old I had fulfilled all the stereotypes of hairy Greek men. Little me had to purchase Gillette razors and shaving cream from the corner shop where I used to play *Street Fighter 2* as the female Asian hairless character of Chun-Li.

After I graduated from high school, I was earning minimum wage, juggling university with no time to shave. The full-grown beard that emerged around my mouth was so thick and black that the men I had more time with asked me what dye I used on it. In the gym, neck-bearded betas side-eyed me. The beard made me a target for the stop-and-search police. You are being randomly searched, Mr Ethno Beard! There I was standing on the platform of the train station trying not to get an erection while Officer Gym Queen patted me down. Always a back and forth, chaser and chased. Once I hid behind a display of Kettle chips when shop attendants spied on me thinking that

I was shoplifting. I wished that they would just stroll up to me in their regulation polyester pants and say, I don't think we have anything for you – you're obviously in the wrong place.

Then I could return triumphantly with shopping bags upon shopping bags, as many shopping bags as there are oranges in a fruit market. I would say to them, Big mistake! Big! Huge!

In the racially charged bullpen of an infants' playground, Bonita Booker told me that boys are spastic made outta plastic. We were hopping on a hopscotch, and just as I landed on the last square I was overcome by the heat and my leg collapsed under me – proving that indeed I was made of plastic. She also called me a wog and pointed to one of her blonde plaits and told me that she was a skip. She schooled me at school. Skips eat meat and three vegetables for dinner. Wogs have mud food.

I walked home that day in tears. And when I came through the door, still crying, I said to Mum, I don't wanna eat mud.

Her hand connected with my face with a *thwack*. She told me to wake up to myself. In the kitchen, she stirred our soup made of twigs and dirt. She told me why we called them skippies. Because they skip through life. Skip on work and skip out on their children. Do your homework and work harder than them and you'll get half of what they have.

My mum did work twice as hard as them. She worked in factories and worked hard to raise me in a world of men that were trying to get her. Eventually her mind skipped out on itself. Thinking about my mum and her mind skipping out made me go to beachside suburbs and eat ice cream on the promenade.

9.

It was mutually agreed upon that we needed to let off some steam after the failure that we had with the Wally campaign. Kane invited two men over and this time there was no need for refreshments. We did need lotions and other paraphernalia.

Before the two strangers arrived, Kane opened a green metal box and showed me the contents. Inside were tiny plastic bags filled with translucent blue shards. He told me he got them at a bargain price because the batch tested badly. I didn't realise there was a factory outlet for meth. We were going to try it out on a guinea pig before we used the product ourselves.

Kane had asked me to shave so our guests would assume that I was white with a tan. You'll seem more trustworthy, he said. He'd invited one 'woggy' guy and thought that would be enough flavour.

The 'woggy' guy was an eager-to-please young bottom. He came into the house with loose steps but his sharp jawline had carefully sculpted stubble. His eyes were solid black and almond-shaped and he told us that he came from a Latinx community and that his name was Pedro.

The other guy was a Kane clone. He wore clothes that would be easy to remove while keeping his sneakers and socks on. He carried a small bag filled with vials. When he arrived, he pointed to the Fred Perry polo shirt that Kane wore and said that he had the exact same one.

Me and Kane sat Pedro down on the couch and asked him to tell us more about himself. He described living in a village during a narco crisis. Drug lords driving around in fortified jeeps. He'd built up his cardio endurance by exercising on the steps of Aztec temples. He waved his hands to illustrate the size of Machu Picchu; he rubbed his neck and the smell of rosewater filled the room.

Kane Clone sat to the side, nodded enthusiastically as Pedro told us about his native cuisine of meats on a stick and how his country had so many favelas. Even though I had skipped high school geography I realised that he had turned Mexico, Brazil and Peru into one country. A search on my phone confirmed this; I showed the results to Kane. Kane Clone asked for a beer and I had to admit that there was only low-calorie hard spirits and room-temperature water. We hadn't thought about getting beer, even though the blue shards of meth were carefully considered.

Me, Kane, Kane Clone and Pedro. We up-downed each other and then the guests inspected our furniture. Kane Clone played Guess the Name of the Modular Sofa. He asked if it was the Valeria model from the Designer Imposter Replika Warehouse. Real Kane said that it was not the Valeria but the Valencia Imperalus model, and they both nodded and uh-huhed and turned their attention to Pedro.

Kane and his doppelgänger occupied Pedro's personal space and looked him over, all the while interrogating him. At one point I glanced over from the kitchen to see the openly Latino tell the Kanes that he was doing a cha-cha-cha dance. He jiggled his hips and it looked more like a belly dance, and those white-bread boys were fooled by the brown skin. Kane kept pushing, but Pedro stuck to his script. Machu Picchu, the Olympics and the cartels. Neither of them cared about his answers. They looked his body up and down, the way he wore his body, and he temporarily distracted them from their office cubicle life. When Pedro's back was turned, Kane smiled and stuck out his tongue at me. He was scheming, his metal box of chemicals waiting to be popped open, a crappy Pandora's box on a discount coffee table.

Every time Kane asked Pedro a question he rubbed his hands over Pedro's T-shirt. First the shoulders, then a thumb across the back of the neck. The boy's body shuddered each time he was touched. Kane threw rapid questions at him. Where were you born? What do you do for work? Do you like it doggy or on your back? Pedro laughed at the last question and both men shuffled closer to him. You can stop with the BS, we know your name isn't Pedro! Kane wrapped his arm around the boy's shoulder and pushed his neck down, putting him in a headlock. Pedro's head was squashed between bicep and forearm; Kane shifted his weight, pulling Pedro's face into his stomach.

Pedro extended his shaved arms and pushed at Kane's body, trying to get away, but Kane kept holding him there. The boy tried to laugh but his mouth was pressed against Kane's shirt. Kane jiggled his arm, bobbing the boy's head up and down. His victim cried, Ooow! and then laughed. Kane Clone pulled out a vial of amyl to sniff. He looked on, adjusting his crotch and grinning. He moved closer to Pedro and lifted his shirt, running his fingers down the ethno twink's side, trying to make him laugh. I watched from the sideline and Kane's voice dropped, became raspy. Go on, tell us ya real name!

Pedro ummed and ahhed. He told us his name was Charlie, and after more and more sways of Kane's plump bicep admitted that it was really Charbel. He wasn't Mexican, Peruvian or Brazilian but Lebanese Maronite. He was born here, second generation, and said that he wasn't *like the other Lebs*. When

Kane's grip on his neck loosened he sat back on the couch and promised to reveal his secret past.

Rosewater Charbel began to tell us his family's origin story. His family came from a long line of purple-dye makers who since ancient times had produced the robes of Mesopotamian royalty. The three of us sat down on the carpet to listen to his story. Rosewater Charbel used his hands to shape the great boats of the Phoenicians, and the top of the glass coffee table was the sea. The boats floated over to an ashtray that represented Malta. In medieval times his ancestors moved to the caves of Mount Lebanon, where they stayed throughout what the West called the Middle Ages and Islam called a golden time. He claimed that his father started the civil war in Lebanon as a child when he lost a pair of dice on the soil of a refugee camp recently set up for displaced Palestinians. Rosewater Charbel turned his digits into guns shooting at each other. He held his hands flat to represent air-to-surface missiles, and did jazz hands to represent the bombs exploding.

While he did an interpretive dance of the civil war we clutched our non-existent pearls and puffed on cigarettes. Kane took out the green metal box. He kneeled beside Rosewater Charbel and put the box in front of him. Kane bowed his head and Rosewater Charbel opened the box. With two fingers he pulled out the glass 'incense burner' with the bulbous tip, a bag of shards and a torch lighter.

The smell of burning plastic filled the room. After the first hit, Rosewater Charbel took off his shirt. His pupils dilated, and a layer of glass fell over his eyes. His lips curled outwards and as his chest heaved, his head rolled up and back. He tried to walk around the living room, but each step made him wobble. His torso stretched and arched. I took a few steps back to take in his writhing body; inside it was a bug trying to escape. I went to grab the paraphernalia and the metal box, but Kane stopped me. He put his lips on my ear and told me that we were still waiting to see what would happen to the test monkey.

Rosewater Charbel undid his button fly. When he could focus for more than a second, he looked at us standing around him. He was breathing deeply – an animal in distress. He took off his tapered jeans and they got stuck around his ankles. Kane Clone approached him and helped him out of his clothes. Wearing his jocks, Charbel started walking in circles around the sofa, looking down at the place where he had sat. His underarms began to smell of the earth. The smell hit us and we all started rubbing parts of our bodies. Kane ran his hands across his chest, Kane Clone tweaked his own nipples, and I put my hands around my neck. Rosewater Charbel darted out of the living room. He ran down the hallway, knocking over lamps, pulling down the framed rainbow flag. We heard the front door slam.

Kane ordered us to collect the boy's clothes so we could go hunt him down. Kane Clone picked up the discarded jeans and found a wallet. He pocketed the dosh and pulled the kid's licence. He had just come of legal age. His name wasn't Charlie or Charbel. His name was the kind of terrorist assemblage you'd see on the news, a hybrid of Abu-El-whatever. The name belonged to a troubled teenager going at it lone-wolf style or the entrepreneur of a halal food truck.

Throughout the night, the young man displayed his three different sexual personae in order of most socially acceptable to least. He had gone from Latino to Phoenician to Muslim and our evening had gone from pre-orgy to story time to chase scene. Kane announced that the night was over, and Kane Clone handed us the boy's clothes. Before he left he placed his hands on our biceps to console us for our loss of dick: Sorry the orgy took a different path and you didn't get your rocks off.

Kane and I took the young man's clothing and went out into the night-time street to look for him. The leaves hung still on the trees; dinner smells wafted out of houses. The streetlights lit up a lone figure in the distance. He had removed his underwear and was standing in the middle of the road, his hands raised to the sky and his head tilted up, speaking to the moon. It must have whispered something back to him, and he took off in the direction of the main road. We ran down the street after him.

A few houses down, I put my arm on Kane's chest to stop him and we talked through our options. Maybe we shouldn't follow him, I suggested – we didn't know what he might do, and we could be dragged into it if the cops came.

Kane agreed but wanted to see the evolving effect of the drugs. We headed back to our place and jumped into his Corolla Hybrid.

Cruising the roads with the windows down, we heard cars beeping somewhere up near the main street. We made our way to the shopping centre and saw the boy standing in the middle of a roundabout. His arms hung down by his sides and swayed around, like they were being blown by an unseen methy wind. We pulled into the shopping centre car park and drove into a spot where we could see the action. Headlights ran over his naked body. For almost a minute he stood statue-still, floodlit by halogen headlamps. One of the trucks turning at the roundabout beeped its horn. The sound woke the statue and he started walking towards the cars circling him. He took three gumby steps, his knees gave way and he fell backwards on the concrete.

Cars stopped and windows were wound down. Arms stuck out of the windows with camera phones pointed in his direction. He stood up again, his head rolling on his neck. His chest heaved and he stepped into the traffic. A white hatchback stopped a metre away from him and flicked on the high beams. There was a blur of movement towards the car, he made his hands into fists and rained three blows on the bonnet, denting it. The sounds of flesh hitting metal made all the traffic stop. He ran to the passenger side and tried to open the door; it was locked, and his nails scratched at the window. The car accelerated, almost sideswiping other cars. The engine revved and the car ran up onto the pavement and into a telegraph pole, its bonnet buckling. Abu-El-whatever had already turned away from the crash and walked back to the roundabout. He stood in the centre and looked up to the sky.

Blue and red lights filled the street. The cops parked and got out of their paddy wagon. Two officers approached him, their arms out, palms facing up. He spoke gibberish at them.

We watched the show from our car. Kane commented on how fucked up Muslim gay boys were but also how hot they were. He mused that the right kind of guy could play a significant role in the campaign against the mosque.

More cops had rolled up; they put yellow police tape around the car that had crashed into the pole. Kane and I watched through the windscreen as Abu-El-whatever got sectioned. Two blue uniforms launched at him, strangled his hands and forced them behind his back. His body contorted, trying to get out of the cops' hold, and they pushed him down on his backside. They were all in the middle of the roundabout and they looked like figures on top of a cake – if it had been made to celebrate police brutality against the mentally ill.

Cars kept circling, slowing down to watch what was happening. Random people had come to watch from the footpath. Young married couples in colour-matched outfits. Middle-aged mothers holding on to their son's necks.

The two cops rolled the boy onto his stomach. Each cop grabbed an arm and they cuffed his hands behind his back. His face was on the ground, then his torso pushed up and he looked to the sky; he flapped up and down, the film of sweat on his naked body making him shine. Red spinning lights joined the scene as the ambulance arrived, driving straight up onto the roundabout.

There was a long silence in the car. Kane gathered the boy's clothes and wallet. He got out of the car, looked around and walked across the car park, then darted over the road towards the onlookers. Kane stalked the edges of the crowd, looking for the right place to enter. I watched Kane move around, dropping the pants, T-shirt and wallet in different areas of the crowd.

When the cops and ambos tried to make Abu-El-whatever stand up, parents covered their children's eyes, shielding them from the sight of his genitals. There was a perversity to this, that they would let their children gawk at a man going through a drug psychosis, watch as he writhed around in distress, but censor his flaccid penis.

Kane got back into the car. He said that he had heard one of the dads warning his kid to stay away from drugs and stay away from Lebs. We watched as two cops lifted Abu-El-whatever by the arms; his legs flopped. The cops pushed him into the back of the ambulance, one cop got in with the ambo and they closed the doors. After a minute the ambulance drove down from the roundabout, the red lights spinning but the sirens off. Traffic began to clear, the energy of the intersection returning to normal.

Two other police officers wandered into the crowd. They were both five-foot-tall Trevor types, dark circles around their eyes, stomachs stretching out their shirts. First they talked to a Dilfy dad standing with his family. One of the Trevor cops pulled out his notepad and started scribbling things down.

Dilfy dad was six foot tall and towered over the Trevor cops; he wore drawstring shorts and had his arm around his teenage daughter's shoulder. She pulled out her phone and showed the officer some video footage. The other cop was walking through the crowd, and he squatted down to pick up the clothes that Kane had discarded. Members of the crowd gathered around him.

We couldn't hear what the girl said to the cop, but she held her hand up to about Kane's height and flexed while gesturing to her shoulders. Preteens on scooters wheeled over to the other cop and pointed in the direction that Kane had gone after dropping the clothes. I looked at Kane: his face was still, his eyes watching the scene. I tapped his hand once and he grabbed my fingers. He started the engine and turned on the headlights. One of the Trevor cops turned around, looking directly at our car. I mouthed, Oh shit, but didn't say it out loud. Kane reversed out of the car park and did a three-point turn. I adjusted the rear-view mirror. The cop watched us drive away, and then he wrote something down in his notebook. There were five or so people standing around the police officer, trying to make out what he was looking at.

We drove silently the long way back to our house. Kane did a reverse park in the driveway. As he reversed, he put his arm behind the headrest of my seat. He turned his head towards me, his face thirty centimetres from mine. The car stopped but the engine still revved. I turned to look at him and he kept his head in the same position. His eyes were glassy; I couldn't read his face. He took his hand off the steering wheel, put the gear in neutral and touched my cheek. He stroked my cheek with the back of his fingers. Kane said that he was pretty riled up.

I didn't flinch and looked him in the eye. Kane laughed and leaned over. His nose was on my nose and he put his lips on mine. We kissed each other for the first time in eons, the drama we'd witnessed on the street powering through our mouths.

Kane got out of the car and came around to open the passenger door. He said that he was riled up because the sex party had been interrupted and because of all the nudity on the roundabout.

He held out his hand to me, and I swivelled my legs around and put my feet on the pavement. Kane pulled me out of the car and into him. His hard tongue darted into my mouth. He pressed against me, moving his hands up and down my back over my clothes. His hands cupped my arse cheeks. It took time to find our kissing rhythm. Once I found the right swirl I opened my eyes.

We were standing under the streetlights outside the house. He said we should go inside, and I said that we could give the married couples and two-point-three families an example of real sex. He grabbed me by the hand and I followed him into the house. He suggested my room and I asked if this meant I would get a discount on my rent.

Kane came into my room and saw the doona strewn over a ball of sheets on my bed. As he pulled me in for a kiss his hands slipped under my shorts, kneading my cheeks and pulling them apart to finger my hole. He pulled off my shirt and bent forwards to breathe in the scent of my armpits. His nose whistled under my armpits and my body jolted, almost getting ticklish. I undressed him and grabbed at the tribal tattoo. He pushed me onto the bed and I looked at him naked, the taut definition of his body. His dick was short, but three fingers thick.

Our skin was wet and we slid against each other. Body odour and the scent of talc mixed in my nostrils. Our crotches were grinding as we kissed, his hands grabbed the back of my knees, pushing them to my ears. It exposed my crack to him and he spat a few times on his dick and guided himself into me. My hole expanded, took him in. I felt every molecule of air against my skin. The smell of Kane was too much, I almost clenched my sphincter onto him, so I focused on breathing through my mouth. My eyes shut themselves and I tried to will them open. A noise began at the base of my body and came out through my lips. Kane hadn't begun to thrust, so I started to move, raising my hips to meet his cock.

During the sex, Kane negged me and it made me more susceptible to him. He would stroke the stubble of my beard, commenting that my hair was so thick that I had dandruff on my face. His finger rubbed in between my eyebrows and it made me conscious of the hairs that I hadn't removed there. Your body is so hairy, he said. But at least you don't have a hairy ass.

The sex ranged from sensual to a series of athletic positions. I could have been in a pump'n'dump car wash or a blow'n'go Slurpee dispenser. My skin became numb to his touch and as a result my brain became deprogrammed to him as a person. Getting used to his body parts in me, getting used to his ideas being inserted into me.

10.

Basil's apartment was in a five-storey building called The Pinnacle, which – of course – he had named. He described it to me using the bullet points from the promotional material, billing it as a series of contained spaces for luxury living in the new Western Suburbs. It was just off one of the main streets in Bankstown, a short walk from the shops.

The apartments on the bottom floor opened into fenced front yards. I pressed the buzzer next to a glass door and a woman's voice answered. I said that Basil was expecting me, and she told me to take the lift to level five. The door clicked open and I walked through the foyer. It smelled of eucalyptus and the floor was made of square ivory tiles. A giant ceramic pot with three giant black twigs rising up to the ceiling stood in front of a giant gilded mirror.

On the fifth floor the elevator opened directly into a large living area. Basil stood waiting for me, shoulders strong. The entire living space behind him was furnished in white with black accents. White leather couches and armchairs had deep seats and high, angular armrests. In front of the sofa was a large television, easily one of the biggest I had seen, and behind it was a glass wall that opened onto a balcony with outdoor furniture in different shades of white. White gloss shelves held a selection of black and white books. Hanging on the walls were silver-framed photos of Basil standing next to his father. In another frame was a youthful picture of his mother, with big bouffant hair and a shiny, blue power dress.

Basil was wearing a blue checked polo, green chinos and three stripe slides. He put his hands in his pockets and asked if I wanted a tour of the place. In the quiet I heard a perfume bottle spritzing. The notes of bergamot and vanilla filled the room and a young woman came down the hallway.

Basil introduced me to his girlfriend, Kamilla. She wore a midriff white top, a white oversized hoodie and ivory track pants. She was barefoot, and her toenails and fingernails were painted the same shade as her track pants. Her skin was too orange, and her straight, pitch-black hair extended all the way down to her waist. She pulled her hoodie across her bare midriff. Picking up on the self-conscious gesture, Basil said, Don't worry about him, honey. He's gay.

Basil told her that I was here to interview him for the book. Kamilla raised a tattooed eyebrow. I walked over to read the spines on the books, all classic literary texts. Some of the titles were in Latin and others in Greek. I asked Basil if he'd read them and he said that the interior decorator got them based on the colour scheme. He asked Kamilla to make us Greek coffee: Make it the way my old man showed you – eh?

I sat down next to Basil on the sofa, pulled out my phone and activated the voice recorder. He sat with one knee up, his thighs almost busting out of his chinos. There was a long silence until Kamilla came back into the room.

She was carrying a clear perspex tray, on top of it were three ivory demitasse cups with gold rims on matching saucers. On a cork mat sat a white porcelain briki and around it were three slender glasses with ice water. Kamilla squatted next to the coffee table, balancing the tray in one hand while setting out the coffees. Look! At! That! Perfect! Hostess! Basil clapped.

Kamilla asked me what kind of books I wrote. I explained that I had published a book of prose poems, and she said that she loved poetry. Her favourite was Rupi Kaur, and through Rupi she had discovered Rumi.

Rupi was the kind of Instagram pop poet that verged more into inspirational self-reflective quotes than poetry;

she was more celebrity than credibility. I told Kamilla the kind of stuff I wrote wasn't that nice, but it didn't matter. She still wanted to read it. Kamila insisted I have the kamaki on top and then poured the coffee. Did many people buy it? she asked. I told her it sold three hundred copies and got a review in the paper. People were ah . . . struck by the images, they were very . . . ah . . . impoverished ah . . . the poor bits of Western Sydney . . . you know. In describing the work, I sounded like a cultural tourist fetishising the place. To break the tension, I said that it wasn't as lucrative as being in property development and property sales and gestured to the apartment. She suggested that I put my poems on Instagram.

On the sofa next to me, Basil moved impatiently. He sat up straight and pushed his chest out. He placed the saucer with the cup on his palm and picked up the cup by its tiny handle with two fingers, his pinkie held out.

Property sales? You think I'm in sales? A salesman? Basil was incensed at the idea that he was no better than a retail store clerk.

Betcha think you're a smug cunt, bro, he said, looking at me side on. Kamilla went to pick up her coffee and then stopped. Basil took a loud sip, drawing out the sound. Betcha read the *Sydney Morning Herald* too and believe all its articles, don't ya? I got your number, bro. You probably wake up every morning, read the *SMH* online, maybe from your phone or even a device.

A device. There was a humour in the way he said device, but it came from anger. Basil raised the cup to his mouth again. His lips were pressed together, and he edged the rim of the cup into them. He tilted the cup and the liquid slurped between his lips. A deliberate slurp to punctuate his monologue.

Betcha look for think pieces or think-pinions on how dumb cunts like me want those dolla dolla bills. Makes ya think, don't it, makes you think about how *oh mi gawd* society is changing or how Sydney is being fucked over by the government and makes you realise that your smarts and poetry make you better than all us money-grubby developers. But I'll tell ya sumthin, no charge. Those shitty little opinion pieces that make you feel smarter about yourself are underwritten by the property section of the paper. Without the real estate market and the ads and the agents there would be no highbrow fucking newspaper. Us grubby developers funded that crappy little review of your book and those three hundred units it moved. Without property developers like me, there would be nothing for you to read, to make yourself feel better than people like me.

His sentence went up at the end, and his last words vibrated. After he'd stopped speaking, he put the cup and saucer down. He stood up and patted down his shirt and went to the glass door to the balcony. He slid it open, letting in the wind and the noise of the traffic, and went and looked over the railing. Kamilla shrugged and said that she still wanted to read my book of poems.

I followed Basil outside. He leaned over the balcony railing, looking down on Bankstown. I apologised for my tone. It was instinctual, like somehow I had been trained to apologise to men when they got angry. Basil said that he wasn't angry, that it was all just a joke.

I joined him looking over the balcony. We looked over all the buildings and streets. We looked over the cranes and empty pits where developments would go up.

Remember all those times when you beat me in class? When you beat me in assignments? said Basil. Felt like shit then but look at me now and look at you.

We looked over train lines and the buses circling. We looked over the whole suburb. In the distance a helicopter hovered above buildings.

Basil unbuttoned the neck of his polo shirt and a thin gold cross fell out; it hung on a chain thicker than the cross itself. The glint caught my eye, and the way the cross fell in the middle of Basil's chest must have made me forget myself – I reached over to take it in my hand. My gesture was more childish curiosity than sultry seduction. Basil put his hand around mine as I clasped the cross. We both froze and heard the sounds of traffic.

You know my ma gave me that, but I got it a new chain, he said. I looked up to his face and his eyelids hung halfway down, his brown eyes looked off into the distance. I let go of the cross and Basil let go of my hand.

11.

Once upon a childhood I was in the bathroom-slash-laundry
and noticed that I had a cowlick on the back of my head.
I scooped up water in my hands and dampened my hair,
patting it down forcefully, but it stood up, erect and militant.
I found my mother's hairbrush in the laundry basket, the
plastic bristles covered with long black strands. A groan came
out of my mouth each time I picked out hairs from the brush.
A golden chain was tangled in the black hairs and I pulled it
out. On the chain was a pendant in the shape of the Greek
island that my mother came from. I put it around my neck
and went to school.

Other students noticed the chain over my collar and asked
me what it was. I said it was an expensive representation of my

ancestral island home. My mum is from an island, stupid! Not the dumb Greek mainland. An actual island. Where people are trustworthy and do as they say.

The gold-plated pendant was in the shape of a hand with three fingers for the peninsulas. As we lined up to go into our demountable classroom, a recently arrived Greek mainlander said that I was wearing a woman's necklace. He said that I might as well get an earring in my left ear and be gay. Watch it! I told him. We islanders are a sneaky bunch.

I grabbed the necklace and pulled it off my neck; the chain snapped, stinging my skin. I put the pendant between my knuckles and swiped at the laughing boys around me. One of the peninsula fingers connected with the mainlander's cheek. As soon as I saw a trickle of blood, I escaped from school and ran home.

Climbing the stairs to our apartment, my feet felt like mountain rocks. I thought I was going to get in trouble for coming home early. Taking the key from under the mat, I opened the door, and heard sobbing in the kitchen.

Aunt Cassie, a family friend, sat at the kitchen table, consoling my mother who had just watched the film adaptation of *Zorba the Greek* like it was the first time. My mother held a semi-gloss photo of the British actor who portrayed our great Mediterranean existential hero. When she saw me, she flung it at me. She put her head in Aunt Cassie's lap and sobbed through a tight mouth, the air whistling between her loose teeth. The photo was at my feet and Aunt Cassie stroked my mother's head with her wrinkled fingers, her gold rings gleaming against my mum's black ponytail. When my mum sat up again, there were two eyeliner rings on my aunty's skirt. Mum told me that she had seen a movie about my father, and I told her that was impossible, because the man playing Zorba was a British actor named Anthony Quinn.

She spat that I was against her too, and Aunt Cassie changed the subject. She asked me why I'd come home, and I said I was sick. Aunt Cassie said she'd known I was coming home early; she had tried to convince my mother of this, but Mum didn't believe her. No one ever believed Aunt Cassie. Not even when she knew who was going to be home next. Not even when she knew which way the wind was going to blow.

Aunt Cassie's jewellery stood out against her clothing like a starry night. Piled on top of her black or navy blouses were always at least three gold necklaces, one with a crucifix, one with a blue evil eye, and another with a locket in the shape of a heart. Up and down her arms were charm bracelets, bangles and cuffs, all in different shades of gold. The combined shininess meant that Aunt Cassie was often attacked by magpies who wanted to steal jewellery to decorate their nests. So Aunt Cassie had learned the best way to fend off bird attacks when walking under trees. Her defence moves made her tough. I knew Mum was safe when they went out shopping for groceries or depilatory creams.

Mum and Aunt Cassie swore by a new product they had seen on TV called Nad's. It was invented by a stay-at-home mum from a Middle Eastern background called Sue Ismiel and named after her daughter Nadine. Aunt Cassie and Mum purchased it as soon as they saw the first infomercial, in which the mother heated up the sticky green goo and then piled it on her daughter's hairy leg. She also applied it to the hair above her daughter's lip and her sideburns. Aunt Cassie and Mum screamed at the television, Oh look! They're just like us! as the mother shared her daughter's indignities and hirsute shame on national television in the spirit of ethnic entrepreneurialism. Sue Ismiel reminded them of the good churchwomen they knew. She was relatable, and they also liked to see a swarthy woman finding success in a country of blondes, bottle or otherwise.

The next day Aunt Cassie came over and pulled a few pots of Nad's out of her fake snakeskin handbag. Mum put towels down on the kitchen floor and stripped down to her bra and knickers. I sat on the couch doing my homework, occasionally turning around to see what was going on.

Mum eased herself down onto the towels. Aunt Cassie got the applicator and spread the green caramel on my mum's hairy leg. She pressed a white strip on the goo and ripped it off; it made a tearing sound. Mum's eyes became steel, her forehead came down and her lips scrunched, her face contorted for battle. In that moment, as a child, I looked at the red marks on her legs and saw them as borders across her body. I remember Aunt Cassie hovering over her, a faithful guide to the green goo. She had foretold that the waxing would cause pain.

12.

I remembered the pre-meth-breakdown couplings between me and Kane, how they happened on and off like some kind of continuous sex flatmate purgatory. When he was bored, he would rub the nape of my neck, or laugh too heartily at my jokes and we would have sex. Then weeks went by with nothing, us being casual flatmates, me telling him in the kitchen that we need toilet paper. He'd find someone else to fuck but if he was bored he would hook up with me again. Regular coupling with Kane was no certified guarantee of intimacy.

Two days after our failed orgy, I woke up alone and naked, the bedsheets had fallen off the bed. This is what flatmates with benefits looked like. My jeans were hanging over the back of a chair, neatly folded, and I was uneasy about this because the previous night Kane had ripped off my clothes and left them on the floor. It meant that he got up during the night, folded my clothes and moved into his room. I remembered the sex Kane and I had had the night before and expected him to be there, lying next to me, perhaps even spooning me.

I walked through the house barefoot, my soles landing softly on the beige carpet. At the end of the hallway I stopped. Kane sat at the kitchen table; the newspaper had been sectioned off into different areas. Sports was laid out next to the social pages, national news separated from world news. In his hands he held the property section. He moved the paper closer to him and then away, back and forth, his forehead wrinkling, distressed about what he was reading. Perhaps even giving a performance for my benefit. I walked up behind him, put my hands on his shoulders and leaned down to peck him on the top of his head. He jolted in shock.

He turned his head to give me a blank stare. Hey? I said to him, part greeting and part question. We had fucked, but Kane was my flatmate-slash-landlord and he wouldn't be able to avoid me by ghosting. I walked to the other side of the table and pulled out the chair. The legs screeched across the floor, Kane kept reading the paper and I asked if there was a coffee pod left for me. He shook the paper to straighten the pages and gestured to the coffee machine, told me there was no milk.

As the Nespresso machine warmed up, I slid the Vanilio coffee pod into the slot and pressed the handle down slowly to lock it in. My back was to Kane at the kitchen table. The patter of Frenchie's feet broke the silence. Usually I would have turned around to watch Kane interact with the dog, but embarrassment filled me because I couldn't understand why the newspaper was more important than me. I heard a chair being pulled out and Kane muttered to the dog, encouraging it to take a seat at the table. I stayed facing the coffee machine, waiting for the light to come on to indicate it was ready; when it did, I pushed the button with my index finger and water gurgled through the machine.

Kane rustled the papers; he let out a groan and a low whistle as he read an article that made him angry. People that express emotions while reading the news are a distinct breed. Kane liked to complain. His whingeing was a weapon. When he'd told me about being raised by a single mother, how poor they were and all the sacrifices she'd made, it was a whinge – that he was at a disadvantage compared to others – but it was also a testament to the inherited strength of character that had helped him overcome adversity. His mother believed in herself! Kane believed in himself! He won the race and got ahead in life! But what he really meant was that others were now behind him and it was their own fault. How he overcame his hard luck in life was a boast, but it was also an attack on those who came last in the race.

In high school Kane studied computers. His technical ability and attention to detail led to an IT course at a technical college. He was a tactile, kinaesthetic learner and his on-the-job learning abilities propelled him quickly up the ladder. His ENTJ Myers-Briggs personality type indicated his decisive leadership skills when, for example, giving coffee orders to underlings or getting someone's ankles behind their ears during sex. As a Sagittarius with Scorpio moon he had a fun, curious approach to work and held long grudges when slighted. With his people skills and knowledge of systems administration, Kane moved into consulting. Big companies would come to him with a problem, a need to update their input and processing points. His skill base included tailoring data entry logistics for the company, but he also knew the right people for systems maintenance.

In office environments, he moved easily between the grunts, the managers and the CEOs. He impressed the grunts by telling them stories about his athletic sex life in a self-deprecating way. Managers were no nonsense and easy to read. CEOs would be approached non-verbally – his body on display, spine straight and shoulders back, legs spread to adjust his height to that of the other person, exhibiting a masculine physicality that was itself a form of communication. Desire and sexuality didn't play a role, but a form of homosocial camaraderie helped. Usually the main guy was fit and healthy, someone who maintained a low percentage of body fat. His body was a representation of his character – noble, not decorative, not vain but practical. Kane kept his body in this fashion. When he picked a shirt for meetings with a CEO, it should be fitted to his skin but not tight enough to be tacky. He regularly met with company boards, and had discovered their recipe. They were mostly men with a token woman, and often an ethnic minority – and this minority performed the ornate social protocols of Anglo culture better than a titled Englishman.

The last drops of black coffee came out of the spout and I took the Bodum double-wall glass to the table. I sat opposite Kane and asked if I could take the social pages. He nodded quickly. The banner headline on the social pages read SIN CITY CONFIDENTIAL. The front page crackled as I turned it over and spread the paper in front of me; the layout was the same as the property section. To escape thoughts of Kane, I burrowed into the pictures and language, gleaning insights into society. There were images of people at events, posing in front of advertisement walls. Shining young women and men, job titles listed next to their names. The launch of a luxury car dealership or the opening of a new licensed venue was cause for celebration. There was even a photo spread dedicated to the release of a pre-mixed alcoholic beverage. The men in the pictures were high shine, wearing blazers that cast their frame into a perfect V. The women were a barrier of teeth and showed patches of glossy skin against the ornate textiles decorating their bodies.

Kane was muttering again. You know, the prices . . . the prices are inclining down nationally, something needs to happen . . . This mosque down the street . . . may be a real problem in the future . . .

I kept looking at the pretty bodies and too-clean teeth. Couples posed together, holding each other in their arms, in a world so far from my experience it might as well have been another country. I took some consolation in the sort of people who made up Sydney high society. The heirs of chicken-factory fortunes and television chefs known for yelling. There were stooped-head footballers and the aggressively blonde. Masc gay couples or metro BFFs were indistinguishable in Sydney society.

Kane wanted to tell me something. He put the newspaper down, came around the table and stood behind me. His fingers grazing my neck changed the energy of the morning. He put his chin on my head and rested his hands on my shoulders. There was a long breath and he spoke: I think I have another idea of how we can stop this mosque.

He had been reflecting on the series of lies Abu-El-whatever had told about his background. We had forgotten his name, and even if we could remember it we probably would have just called him Gulf Bottom or Dune Slut. That boy was a changeling to us, and it gave Kane the idea of how flexible identities could be. He had been pondering how all the gay wogs he met were just as fucked up as Abu-El-whatever. I told him that sounded racist, but he said that Aussie gay men were fucked up in a different way. I asked him to explain.

Hiding. Hiding is why. The numerous gay wogs he had slept with hid who they were. If they didn't hide from everyone, they at least hid from some people. Kane pointed out that before we found out that Abu-El-whatever had a Muslim name, he pretended to be Latino and then Christian Lebanese.

Sam was another example to illustrate Kane's fucked-up gay wog thesis. Sam was short in stature and thought that there was something more going on between him and Kane than there was. He was married happily to a lesbian in a sham arrangement, and he told Kane about the joy between him and the lesbian wifey: We let each other cheat. And she's femme, so I get to dress her up!

Once Sam was having a threesome and his in-laws came to visit, which meant that hilarity ensued.

I told Kane that Sam sounded happy even if he wasn't authentic.

Kane pulled out a chair next to me and sat down facing me. I put down the Sin City Confidential. I was uncomfortable because he kept using the word 'wog'. Kane told me another story about a time he needed peen, so he picked up a dude in a dashiki and gave him a blow job behind an Awafi chicken shop. Later that day Kane saw the guy with a wrapped-up wife. The wife was pushing a pram with multiple children tethered to it. I told him that the dashiki dude was probably bi. Kane said, Bisexuals don't exist. It's a marketing concept.

There was a story about another man he dated, a total freshie from the Middle East. The guy was eight foot tall and weighed over a hundred kilos of CrossFit muscle. According to Kane he had lovely inflated nipples on top of a lovely inflated chest. Lovely muscles! The guy told Kane that he had been blown to Australia by the funky Arab desert winds and his mission in life outside of managing a hedge fund was to teach the world how to belly dance.

He had an Instagram account dedicated to his butt. His butt in thongs, his butt in jockstraps, his bare butt in Bali, his jockstrap butt in Bali. Apparently, ex-Wahabi CrossFit went to the police to apply for an apprehended violence order against his Serbian ex-boyf, and an Officer Trevor type threw his arms in the air and belly laughed him out of the station. Officer Trevor said, Bwa ha ha ha ha! He'd need protection from you! Not the other way around! But the way ex-Wahabi CrossFit explained it, he hoped to get the AVO so the other guy wouldn't out him. Summarising his thesis, Kane concluded that the extremity of the gay wogs' situation and their lack of sexual freedom, created a powder keg of fucked-upness, which resulted in their doing extreme kickboxing, belly dancing and butt-themed Instagrams.

Kane's cheeks were flushed and he had started to breathe more heavily. He told me about the amazing squats ex-Wahabi

CrossFit could do in the bedroom because of his flexible legs. Apparently, thanks to belly dancing he had a waist that moved independently from his torso. Kane paused and licked his lips. He picked up his phone and made a booty call to ex-Wahabi CrossFit.

I sat there like a lump as Kane talked on the phone. He asked his old fuck buddy how he was doing, Kane nodded uh-huh uh-huh and then his voice changed to a caramel-salted sleaze. Kane requested his presence, I could hear the light buzzing of the other guy's voice.

I put my hands to my arms to see if I was there. Ran the back of my index finger on my thigh, to make sure that I hadn't become an object in the house. Kane kept talking on the phone, arranging a time to meet and I felt as numb as the Eames replica Eiffel dining chair that I sat on.

I decided to take the dog for a walk. As I put the harness on Frenchie the French bulldog, I realised that Kane had never got around to telling me his idea of how to stop the mosque.

⊞

The neat shrubs watched me as I walked along the grass of the nature strip. Frenchie's paws made a *tap tap tap* on the pavement. All along the street the houses were spaced equidistant from each other, all painted in variations of the same colours, and kept repeating, repeating, repeating.

When I got home a pair of hi tops guarded the front door. Stepping into the house, I could hear Kane making a noise that was more yell than grunt. I stopped at his bedroom door and put my ear against the wood. There were two distinct voices, shouts verging on screams. Underneath these voices, thumping sounds combined with squeaks from the bed. It was more experimental opera than sex; I expected the door to open and two nude figures in goat masks to come out and dance around a yellow hazard sign. I rested my forehead on the door and shut my eyes, imagining ex-Wahabi CrossFit lying under Kane, his stomach on the bed, while Kane was on top of his bumpy, muscled back penetrating the mounds of round, brown flesh and going from white to pink to red.

One thing I wouldn't miss was Kane's orgasm face. When he was about to cum, his chin retracted all the way back into his neck, and his lips and eyes disappeared. As he exploded over my chest I would stare at his beetroot face, until he was just a head of hair on a flesh pole.

I stood there listening to the sex and I remembered the many times Kane had thrust into me. I had thought each thrust was a step towards a life together in the kit house with the replica designer furniture. We would share three-hundred-thread-count sheets and he could complain when I left my Converse in the wrong place. I could have been happy with Kane, grown old with his leathery neck and upper-range

IT life. The grunts and woofs coming through the door were bombs dropping on my suburban aspirations.

⌗

I decided that a mute protest was the only response. For three days I didn't speak to Kane and he didn't notice. Ex-Wahabi CrossFit was still around and I bumped into him coming out of the shower. He had a towel around his waist and was exactly as Kane described. Big nipples on big pecs. Muscles on muscles, and I had to crane my neck to talk to him. The hair on his body was millimetres long, thick and stubbly, little spikes growing back after a waxing, ingrown hairs ruining a perfectly good chest. I introduced myself. His accent sounded French. He had a floating lisp and a deep voice but an excitable tone, the sound of his voice was an impaired masculinity.

Being ethno gay myself I knew the parameters for conversation. I knew never to ask, Where do you come from? Or, Who are your people? So we just stood in the hallway, me leaning on a wall while I asked about his day. I was overly nice to hide my jealousy. At the end of our conversation he shook my hand vigorously, perhaps overenthusiastically as well. He slipped back down the hallway and a few minutes later the experimental opera started up.

Three days later, I saw him one more time. Ex-Wahabi CrossFit was sitting in the living area, his arm on the back of the sofa. He wore a tank top and a thick smell came from his armpits. I gulped and felt the blood pouring into my lips. He shook my hand and asked if I wanted to have dinner with him and Kane. My one-man boycott of Kane had collapsed because I didn't have that big Scorpio grudge energy. At dinner Kane broached the idea of ex-Wahabi CrossFit being a spokesman against the mosque. He told us to go fuck ourselves.

13.

Throughout the 1980s and 1990s, Mary Kostakidis was a stern-faced, shoulder-padded newsreader and an idol to the Greek women of Australia. She was the original gangsta of the multicultural public TV station SBS. Never a bad word was said about her by the Greeks, even though Greeks are notorious badmouths.

The first time I heard Mary's voice I was doing homework in my room when her low register came floating through the apartment. I walked to the lounge room and a shot of her head and torso appeared on the television. I stood looking at the screen. Her thick brown hair was expertly presented in cascading rolls. A tailored red blazer fitted her perfectly. I said that I liked her red blazer and brown hair and Mum waved a hand at me and said that she knew everything about her.

Mary was one of the smartest women in the community. She spoke the best Greek and English in this whole country. I briefly wondered if she wore the perfume Tabu – my mother's scent – but because she was such a high-class lady I decided she probably had a bottle of YSL Opium in her dressing room. I imagined her hand around the maroon bottle and how she would dip an index finger with a red nail into the liquid and trace the scent on her neck and wrists like Linda Evangelista did in the commercial. Unlike the commercial, I didn't picture her in a post-apocalyptic landscape surrounded by men in loincloths because I had too much respect for her. When the fantasy ended I stood in front of the TV and asked my mum what kind of perfume Mary Kostakidis wore, and Mum threw an old phonebook at my head. The phonebook landed next to the second, non-working TV that was in our living room.

Mary's nightly TV presence was one of many ways in which we Greeks were coming to prominence. Another part of this renaissance in Australia was comedy theatre shows. I once begged Mum to take me to the theatre; my pre-teen gay brain thought that I would be watching men in tights holding skulls or Polacks ripping off their tight white T-shirts. My mum, not suspecting where my real interests lay, took me to a play called *The Wogs Must Be Crazy Two*. I expected tiered seating and red wine but what I got was Marrickville Town Hall, where a big banner read THE WOGS MUST BE CRAZY TWO: THIS

TIME IT'S WOGGIER! in a cartoon font, accompanied by iconic images of Greek culture such as the Parthenon and a Holden Monaro. Most people wouldn't have called it theatre because of the souvlaki stand out front, but I was happy.

The show was a series of skits and monologues. One man dressed up as an old Greek yia yia. Seeing a man wearing a bouffant wig and dressed in a black dress and fringed shawl was enough to make people laugh even before he spoke. When he did speak in the voice of the yia yia he dropped the register of his voice and frayed the edges of his sentences. In a gruff war-worn voice he said things that a Greek grandmother would say, like: My grandchildrenz don't know how work is, they lazy with Walkmanz and Michael Jacksonz, they no even know how to use knife to stab a soldierz neck.

All the young members of the audience laughed at the references to contemporary culture, and the older members of the audience laughed at their memories of the American- and British-sponsored civil war. I laughed along with both groups and looked for cues to laugh from the older gener-ation, pretending that I understood what it was like to live under an occupied Greece. My mum laughed so hard that she rocked back and forth, slapping her thigh. When we got home she lifted her skirt and showed me the red marks just above her knee.

Once, I sat on my bed and drew three sirens on a rock. Mum had recently told me the story about women that used their voices to kill men so I wanted to render them. I used three different shades of blue Faber-Castell pencils to draw the sea – an aqua colour for the area around the rocks, a denim-blue pencil for the main part and navy to show the deep scary parts of the sea. I sharpened the tips as much as possible and angled the pencil to cover the largest area. And then Mum yelled at me from the living room. Her voice came through the walls and each syllable shook me.

When I heard her voice, my eyes became blank and my body moved without thinking. She yelled that it was Thursday night and I should immediately stop what I was doing and get in there. I threw my pad and three blue pencils on the bed and ran to the living room. I pulled one of the many mismatched cushions off the couch, put it under my bum and sat at her feet. She turned on the TV; it stuttered with static, and she got up and hit the set a few times. We were ready to watch our favourite TV show, *Who Let the Wogs Out?*

The people who made *Who Let the Wogs Out?* were the same people who created the theatre show *The Wogs Must Be Crazy One & Two.* The show was set in a family-run fish and chip shop. There was a glamorous but useless young son; the daughter was aggressive but confused. Me and Mum would sit on the couch and eat cheese and onion Smith's chips and laugh at their jokes. Their jokes included mangled versions of English sayings, for example: Two birds in the bush are good but it's better to have two birds in the nightclub wearing short skirts. The daughter was called Koula and her voice had that deep, raspy quality that I associate with Greek women.

There is Koula from *Who Let the Wogs Out?* or the yia yia from *The Wogs Must Be Crazy Two*, there is even Mary Kostakidis from the news, all of them with those deep, sonorous voices. Now every time I hear the low register of a Greek woman's voice the land gives way to the sea and I am in the water, swimming towards them, as they call me home.

14.

I lay on my side in bed, my hand under the pillow, replaying
the long interview I'd conducted with Basil in his apartment.
His voice boomed out of the phone speaker beside my head.
Being in the presence of Basil's booming voice and charis-
matic gestures made me feel like I had witnessed a theatrical
performance. I carried the feeling over to what I was doing
the next day. If I temporarily forgot about him, all I needed
was to smell Greek coffee or listen to his voice and there he was
again, revving his Mustang and driving too fast through a
roundabout.

When we were in the apartment, Basil popped against the
monochromatic décor. By contrast, in her white hoodie and
ivory pants, Kamilla seemed an extension of it.

Kamilla looked like the other young women in the Western Suburbs. They had long black hair down to their waists; it was naturally long, but straightened flat like a sheet. The hair was obviously thickened by extensions – a too thick black column going down their back. They had contoured pancake-makeup that became chalky and runny as the day wore on. Their lips were snails around their mouths. I'd seen them lining up at McDonald's in the food court, delicately pulling a snakeskin wallet from an oversized Louis Vuitton bag, trying not to break their Day-Glo stiletto nails.

This form of drag, so successfully normalised through pop culture, culturally merged all the young women into one. These young women were no longer Christian or Muslim. Arabs became Greeks became Africans became skips, all of whom became Kardashianettes. When I walked through the food court and saw them loitering, I wondered if those girls were copying the Kardashians or if perhaps Kim herself had set up cameras in the change rooms of the clothing boutiques of the Western Suburbs, so she could steal their style.

The straightened hair, claw nails, clothes streamlined against skin and makeup caked on to faces made them appear to be in their thirties. But when I heard their first girlish WTF! or ohmigod really! as they chewed gum, I realised they were youthful and immature.

Although Kamilla shared the aesthetic sensibility of the Kardashianettes, she was different to the rest of them because she seemed mature. She didn't find me interesting or a novelty act because I was gay – if anything, I sensed that she was suspicious of me. Kamilla didn't use her laughter to mask her anxiety, she didn't giggle when she almost overfilled water in a glass, she didn't snicker when I tripped over the cowhide rug in Basil's study.

This maturity was surprising in someone who subscribed to the aesthetics of the mass consumer zeitgeist. And, as a gay man, I always had a fascination with commercial feminine beauty and how it requires hours of unseen labour to maintain.

Basil had found a perfect mate, but I needed to know more about her. There was a calm to her, a steadiness that I had not encountered in the women of my own life.

I kept on listening to Basil's voice while I lay in bed. The speaker on my phone had picked up the sounds in the background. Sounds made by Kamilla herself. The slap of her slides as she walked across the floor, even water being poured into glasses. I heard her laugh when Basil confessed that he wore Davidoff Cool Water cologne in high school. During a lull in conversation Kamilla asked us boys if everything was okay.

In the interview, I asked Basil about his first memory of home. He said that he remembered his dad building a treehouse for him.

I asked when that happened. Basil said that his father went away for a period after his mother died. For a long time Basil was raised by his aunty.

I asked why his father went away. Basil said that his dad went to Greece to grieve. When his dad came back, he built Basil a treehouse and it was his first memory.

⌗

I pushed the buzzer outside Basil's apartment building. Kamilla's voice came out of the speaker box, the metal grille giving it a frenzied quality. She told me to look at the camera. I looked through the glass doors and up around the awnings, then finally saw it above the buttons on the buzzer, a discreet shiny black dot. With my face so close to the camera she would have been able to see every mole and oversized pore.

Previously, I was having coffee with Basil when he got an SMS from her and looked up to the sky and sighed. He said that he was going to marry that girl. I asked if they would have a Greek Orthodox wedding and my arms stiffened when he said Kamilla would have to convert. I told Basil that I already thought she was Greek, but apparently she was a skip, from the Northern Beaches of Sydney. I didn't believe him. Kamilla did things and wore things that I thought belonged purely to migrant culture. Once, I was with Basil at his apartment when Kamilla came in holding a box of cakes from Sweet Fantasy, which is the only place in Sydney for Greeks to buy desserts. It's the kind of place you only know about through generational knowledge. We both stood up to greet her and she just looked at me, put the box of cakes in my hands and then turned her attention to putting her handbag away. Her familiarity with me, such a dominant move, was pure bossy wog girl. I didn't believe Basil when he told me she was a beachside blonde Aussie.

To prove it, he brought up her social media feed and showed me a photo of her from when she was in high school – thin lips and strawberry blonde hair, her face covered with freckles. I took the phone out of Basil's hand and swiped through the pictures.

In another high school photo Kamilla wore a shapeless blue tunic. Her hair was parted on the side and tucked behind her ears. I flicked through more recent photos, looked at her thick, waist-length black hair with the centre parting, her freckled skin covered with concealer and foundation. Her painted face looked different in each photo, and I realised she was experimenting with contouring. In a selfie taken in a marble bathroom she was wearing a tailored blue blazer, her cleavage exploding out of a white blouse, and her cheekbones looked higher than usual. In another selfie, wearing all black, she stood in front of a coffin and her nose looked much slimmer; she had captioned this photo #sad. But the biggest spot-the-difference was her lips. She had gone from modest slithers in her high school photos to plump slugs – splat! – across her face. People call these injectable-filled things duck lips, but beaks are never painted in colours like Rouge Noir or Girl on the Town Red.

The elevator carried me up to the apartment and opened straight into the living room. A black folio and an open laptop sat on the white coffee table. I called a Hello? It echoed through the apartment and Kamilla called back from the bathroom. She said she was just adding touches to her face and she would be done soon.

I walked down the hall, wanting to have a look at the complex ritual of applying makeup. The door was open, and she stood at one of the twin vanity units. Pots and tubes and brushes were laid out in front of her. Bright lights around the mirror lit up her face. She applied liquid concealer and smoothed it out with a sponge. I looked beyond her black column of hair and zoomed in on her face. There was a blue bruise on the left side that went from the top of her cheek to her eyebrow.

It was a walked-into-a-door bruise, it was a his-hit-felt-like-a-kiss bruise. I almost dropped my bag.

One side of her face was already covered with concealer and she was trying to paint over the bruise. Her mouth froze when she noticed me standing in the doorway. She moved only her eyes to look at me, and told me to wait in the living room, her voice efficient. I was a staff member given orders.

The sight of her bruise made me stumble away from the door. I went to the sofa and sat down and breathed in the new leather smell. The apartment was as crisp as a cloudless cold day. The tiles had a Windex shine. The floor-to-ceiling windows to the balcony gleamed, reflecting the white interior of the apartment. The gloss coffee table glowed, except for a new scratch almost the length of my arm, running under the laptop and folio.

Kamilla eventually emerged from the hallway, a thick sheen of foundation over her skin. Her eyelashes were insect legs. Her face was steel, emotionless.

She got me a glass of water and asked about my day. Her track pants were figure-hugging three stripes and she wore a matching Adidas shirt with the logo across her breasts. She sat next to me and put one leg up on the sofa. Her toenails were rounded off with a grey French tip.

Before I turned on the voice recorder on my phone I asked Kamilla if there was anything she wanted to tell me. I told her that I would keep her secret, or maybe even talk to Basil for her if she wanted. She leaned back into the deep seats of the sofa. She looked around her apartment and said: Sometimes you make people hit you, because you use words that give them no other option. I picked up the glass of water and took a sip.

Is this what you are used to? I asked her, Was your dad like this? She said she didn't know. Her parents got divorced when she was in kindygarden and she went to live with her grandmother on the Northern Beaches. I asked for more information about the divorce. What happened?

She said her mother disappeared, went to live her own life. Kamilla stood up to pour water out of a stainless-steel jug into my glass. The water fell from a height, creating a column.

Kamilla told me about her comfortable upbringing on the Northern Beaches. Packing her towel in her schoolbag every morning. Days spent lying around on the sand. Beachside boys with perma-salt scent, peeling wetsuits off their skin. Beachside there were no Basils, no boys with souped-up cars. The few wogs she encountered had adopted Australian ways. They were laid-back, never raising their voices, and dressed in that casual, muted way that beach culture demands.

She dropped out of school early and the only job she could find was a receptionist in a hairdresser-slash-beauty salon in Parramatta. When she showed up for her first day of work, she had shoulder length blonde hair and a sensible pink blazer. As the beauty technicians came into work that day, she looked at their long, perfectly straight hair and spray orange-tinted tans. She saw herself through their eyes: A naive little pink-skinned Aussie wearing a pink blazer. All pink and vulnerable.

Armour, Kamilla called it; the girls at the salon taught her an armour.

Kamilla came under the mentorship of Sonja – the chief cutter and colourist at the salon. She taught Kamilla the intricacies of how to be a boss bitch and how to perfect the ornate decorations that accompanies the attitude. Kamilla said 'boss bitch' in a loud, aggressive tone, landing each syllable, her cadence adopted from the OG girls of Western Sydney. Sonja had extended and coloured Kamilla's hair, shown her the right shade of concealer to cover her freckles. She taught her how to layer different shades on her cheekbones to give her face a more angled look, and the right highlight to use on the bridge of her nose to make it more prominent. I looked at Kamilla's face with its carefully contoured angles; the soft Aussie girl with the MIA mum was gone.

I knew that my reflections on Kamilla were just superficial, I knew that the artifice she constructed around herself was a way to obfuscate people. She loved to misdirect, especially when I asked her about the motivations and relationships that drove her. When I asked about the first time she met Basil, she told me what she was wearing that day – a lime-green singlet top. I asked how she had been affected by her mother leaving. She said she hoped her mum was okay. Whenever she was satisfied with an answer she sat back on the white leather sofa and scanned the room. I asked Kamilla why she did this interview. She shrugged, said that Basil made her.

I looked for the bruising I had seen in the mirror but couldn't find a trace. The concealer and foundation had turned her face into one colour. She took a clump of her hair and ran her fingers through the glossy black lines. One of the strands of hair floated down to the couch. I reached for it and picked it up between my two fingers, like when I picked the strands of my mother's hairs out of a brush.

A vision of my own mother standing at the front of our old apartment filled my mind. Her round face and her fingers running through strings of her own black hair. She was in a faded red shirt that she wore as a dress. The letterbox next to her was spewing paper. The recycling bins were overflowing with rubbish. Kamilla asked me where I was. I shook my head and came back to the white luxe apartment. My legs stuck to the leather.

15.

In my twenties, when I had youthful and plump skin, I was sitting in a lecture at university when I realised that I had a voicemail from my mum. I bent down under the desk and put the phone to my ear. She urgently needed to see me. I left class straight away and hopped on a bus that took me a few streets from the old apartment block where we used to live together. When I walked into the complex, I looked up to the fourth floor and saw her standing on the balcony. She had both of her arms in the air, waving them around to a song that only she could hear.

I hadn't lived with her for a year – I was crashing in a share house – and as my Tigers stepped on the carpeted stairs, I steadied myself for the crap in her place.

My keys were in my hand and I unlocked the door. In the front room, most of the furniture had been removed. I sighed and moved through the apartment. A television sat on a box in front of a tatty sofa, and the table lamp was on the floor. Dust on the lampshade, dust on the light globes, dust on top of the television. The sun shone through the windows, the grime making shapes on the glass. Old newspapers were stacked knee-high all over the living room. Bills were piled up next to the door. One wall was covered with post-it notes and they were grouped in clusters. When I stepped closer, I saw that each cluster had words written in Greek and English. The words were masculine adjectives, a list of physical attributes of a certain man and then places that she had seen that man. It seemed like she was taking notes on the men who she thought were stalking her and then grouping them into clusters.

Mum was still on the balcony. I slid open the glass door and asked her what was going on. As she turned around her breasts almost spilled out of the ripped neckline of her faded purple T-shirt. In each hand she held plastic white posies. Look at me! All the men look at me! But I love these!

I squinted my eyes and scratched my head, let out a sigh. With her right hand she lifted the plastic flowers above her head. She said that she had called me to show me the flowers in the sunlight and was glad I came before night fell. She offered one to me, twirling it in her fingers.

It's difficult to explain in English the concept of mental health to Greeks of the diaspora, because of the way that their language froze. A term that is often used to describe mental illness in the Greek community is *Psihiki Igia*. *Psihiki* means the soul, *Igia* means health. Health of the soul implies that there is something spiritually wrong with the individual, and it stigmatises the person's inherent being. That ancient Greek man, Socrates, with his healthy mind-slash-body theory, was a smug bastard.

Mum gave me the flowers and I held them in my hand. I asked if that was the only reason she had called me. She went inside and sat on the couch, and I followed her. I squeezed the flowers in my fingers and the plastic cut into my hands. I tried to make her understand that she had called me during university and I had skipped out on class. She slid her head down on the couch and said that I was just like all Greek men.

You are all the same, you are those plastic flowers and your father was a plastic flower too! Mum kept repeating this, and I offered to make her a cup of tea. I went into the kitchen and turned on the kettle. As the steam rose from the spout it made me sad to think that I belonged to a category of men who are plastic flowers.

There weren't many Greek men in my life. One Father's Day when I was in primary school I asked my mum who my dad was. She said it was better I didn't know who he was or what kinds of things he did. It was for my own sake.

We were going for a walk together and I was holding her hand. I was scared she was going to do the bolt. I didn't ask again. But I remember that when she said that it was better I didn't know, she stared down at the path. Her brows hardened, and her lips pressed together. She squeezed me hard and was silent for the rest of the way. When we got to school, she let go of my hand. It was white and numb, and as I ran into the playground I shook it a few times to get the blood flowing again.

Another time in primary school, we each had to give a speech in class about our parents. Harry Hippopoulos spoke about his father's job as an electrician. He told us about his dad's tools and the box that he carried them in. His dad drove a white van with his name on the side. Harry was proud of his dad and even talked about spending afternoons playing soccer with him. Afterwards we could ask questions. I asked Harry what his mum did, and he said that she did nothing. The teacher queried Harry further about his mother, and Harry said that his mother took care of the home.

When it was my turn I uncrossed my legs and stood up in front of the class. My notes were on an A4 piece of paper. I told the class that once my mum had worked in a factory where they made custard powder. Her job was to clean the vats where the product was mixed. I described the size of the vats, they were as wide as a room and two storeys high.

Mum would come home wheezing and the doctor diagnosed her with industrial asthma and then she had to give up her job. It was Harry who yelled out that my mum was a dole bludger. I didn't know what that meant. The teacher shuffled me away and didn't let the class ask me any questions.

That afternoon, I saw Harry Hippopoulos leaving school with his dad. I walked up to say hello. Harry's dad had thick legs and a fresh haircut. Below his dyed-black hair his face was heavily tanned. I told Harry that I liked his speech, and his dad ruffled Harry's hair and winked at me. They held hands and walked out of the school gate. I followed them and asked what we were going to do now. Harry's dad turned around and said, We're going to our home and you should go to your home now.

Because I didn't have men in my life, I assumed all fathers were like Harry's dad. When I went home that day, I replayed in my mind the wink, the ruffle of the hair, the blue shorts and the cheerfully hairy legs of Harry's dad.

The next day was our teacher's birthday. I went to school early so I could see Harry's dad drop him off. When they came around the corner, Harry held a large plastic posy for the teacher. I asked him where he got it from and he pointed to his dad.

16.

I spent too much time in the mirror getting rid of the stray hairs sprouting on my face, mostly on the top part of my cheek but also coming out of my ears.

After a shower I put on jean shorts frayed above the knee and an oversized sleeveless tee. The whirr of the NutriBullet drew me to the kitchen. Kane stood in front of the appliance, looking at it with the focus of someone mapping out an attack. When he saw me, the first thing he said was that my sleeveless shirt was an inappropriate garment to wear to a picnic with his work friends. I told him it was good to know that somebody who tested meth out on strangers still had sartorial standards for professional events. On the kitchen bench a Kahlua and a Stoli bottle rose up like two giant cocks. Next to them was a bag of ice that was melting, the water spreading across the bench, trickling under a Greek tin of Nescafé.

Coffee frappes are a classic Greek summer drink made in a milkshake maker, using a special type of instant coffee that has been manufactured for whipping. The coffee powder is mixed with milk or water, and then spun around to create a thick frothy drink. Mum tried to make frappes in a bowl with a fork, but it just caused a mess, coffee water sprayed on our T-shirts and kitchen curtains. Kane had told me that he got a taste for the drink when he wore speedos in Mykonos, and when he got back to Australia he set out to master it. He had modified the recipe by adding liquor to replicate the glorious alcohol-and-caffeine hit of espresso martinis.

Kane handed me the icy black drink in a tall Poco Grande glass with a metal straw. We went to his bedroom to decide what shirt he would let me borrow. He muttered to himself about finding something more a-propro. I told him that a-propro wasn't a word and Kane's face was deathly serious.

We were going to a picnic with nine-to-five corporate gays. These were the gayelles who lived the dream of an apartment in the city and homes in the country. They had already taken a shine to Kane and, if they shone brightly enough, there could be great things coming his way – holidays in the rolling hills and a finer class of recreational designer mood-constructers (which were just drugs with more dollar signs attached to them and a veneer of respectability). Getting in with them required putting on a grey button-down shirt, open to reveal my sleeveless tee underneath. Kane threw a baseball cap at my head. I went to the bathroom. Under the bathtub faucet I washed the muck out of my hair and put it on. The hat had a grey and pink paisley pattern that complemented my shirt, making it look as if I had planned my outfit.

⊞

The Uber dropped us off at the start of the botanic gardens. The sea salt from the harbour made the air crisp. I wondered out loud how long it would be until the government found a way to privatise this land and turn it into apartments. If that happened, Kane said, I would *-just-* adore to buy a harbourside apartment. I raised my hands in the air, exhausted. Part of me thought, Fuck it, I hope they do sell this gorgeous flora-filled publicly accessible land and turn it into a casino; the only people who come here anyway are branded office-lunch-hour joggers. When the next recession hits, those hot corporate runstagrammers can get employment turning tricks outside the casino.

We walked down a road lined with trees and past the cliff formation known as Lady Macquarie's Chair. Kane pointed to the rocks and said he didn't know who Lady Macquarie was, but her seat didn't look too comfortable.

Joggers came at us from all directions. On one side of the path was the open-air cinema, but I kept looking out to the harbour. Boats were scattered across the cove, all positioned for a prime view of the Sydney Opera House. I watched people on the deck of a party boat. They held out their smartphones, extending their arms as far as possible to capture their faces, champagne flutes and the harbour behind them. They didn't look like the floating rich; they were office schlubs who had hired the boat for a work party. If I squinted I could make out their outfits. They had chosen clothes they thought looked nautical, such as blue-and-white-striped long-sleeved shirts and fisherman's caps. I couldn't see their feet, but I assumed boat shoes had been purchased for this team-building event. The women wore all white. As they drank orange liquid out of flutes and posed for their photos, the harbour rolled out and the sun shone on it only for the revellers.

The gays we were meeting had secured prime real estate in the gardens. Their set-up overlooked the harbour and was shaded by a fig tree, its enormous branches reaching over the rugs, baskets and eskies. They clocked Kane and started waving us in.

As we got closer I saw the sharp colours that they wore. Me and Kane were looking extra: we had got picnic casual wrong, mistaking the event as dressier than it was. The men wore jorts and Hi Top sneakers with tank tops, the armholes draping all the way down to their waists, exposing their lat muscles and hips. Their jean shorts – matchy matchy – were cut to just above their knees but frayed at the seams. The older one introduced himself to me as Aleks, pronouncing the *ks* with a Yugoslavian edge. I raised my eyebrows in surprise and asked Aleks if he was Macedonian. He shook his head. He'd changed the spelling of his name, he said, pre-emptively answering my question, so his résumé would stand out more – Aleks is a bit more of a banger than Alex!

Beside him stood his partner, Eduardo. There was a younger lilt to his voice, and he would only begin his sentences when his partner had finished. He had brown glowing skin, thick black eyebrows and the short stature of a South American. To make conversation I thanked him for allowing me to come to the event. After a brief silence he asked if I would like to connect with him on social media.

Aleks was an older version of Eduardo, something Eduardo would eventually turn into if the right amount of amyl nitrate was added. It seems to be de rigueur for a male homosexual in need of a partner to find one who can go full twinsie. After a life in gay land I was used to it, but something made me flinch in their presence. My head gave involuntary short shakes and I realised that I was overcome with the sublime. Although I had encountered numerous couples who looked alike, the effect is uncanny when boyfriend twins are neither the same age nor the same race. Both had animal tattoos on their right shoulders. No doubt their self-declared spirit animals. Their hair was cropped short, and their office-job paunches had been corrected with lots of wide-grip seated cable rows. Their legs were hairless and smooth with a slightly orange glow. Kane had met Aleks at the water cooler in a finance company and if I didn't know this I would have assumed that these two men, with their epic baseball caps and on-trend tattoos, were athletic go-go dancers or the respectable type of entrepreneurial escort.

Aleks asked my name, and I told him it was Pano. He said that I looked like one of the husbands on *Real Housewives of Sydney*. I dared to ask which one and he lightly slapped me on the shoulder with a broken wrist. Stop it! he said, laughing. And I looked around me, at Aleks, at Kane, and had déjà vu. I asked, Stop what?

After the introductions, we all sat down. A silence descended on us, broken by a speedboat whirring across the water. Kane had taken a seat near Aleks and I was left on the other side of the food spread with Eduardo. Everyone stretched out their legs and I reached for the blanket to cover my hairy pins.

Our hosts gestured to the food laid out on the blanket. A platter displayed blueberries and slices of watermelon, oranges, bananas and honeydew lined up in rows. It resembled a rainbow flag, and it wasn't an accident. When I enquired about the fruit, I learned that those weren't bananas but plantains. Bananas have a high glycaemic index, silly! There were two small plates of cheeses with a packet of activated charcoal water crackers next to them. I looked over at Kane sitting next to Aleks; they mirrored each other's body language, both sitting on their knees with their feet tucked under their backsides. They were talking about the new data software Kane had installed, and Aleks would reach over and touch Kane on the shoulder or bicep when he made a point.

We were part of a lovely gay world where we could fuck our flatmates, feel nothing about sex and then go to parties with each other. We reserved our excitable feelings for signature cocktails and the right clothing. This brave new world of comfortable sex and indifferent relationships was my home. We knew physical sensations, the comfort of a sex partner's body and remembering the feel of their hands on our lower back.

Kane and Alex were flirting so I shrugged it off and looked at Eduardo. Eduardo asked the loaded question about what I did for a living. I considered answering honestly; I lived a meek writer's life in the burbs, scraping by on articles and copywriting jobs, barely keeping my head above water. That I was writing a biography of a guy I thought I hated, and that I mostly procrastinated. I wanted to tell him that I work or I die – that I have to work to pay the rent, so I can have a place to sleep, buy antibiotics if I get the flu and eat food that I haven't fished out of a dumpster. Instead I told him that I wrote things here and there, and he sliced off some brie and put it on a black circle that was supposed to be a cracker.

If someone asks what you do for a living within the first five minutes of meeting them, you can be assured that they

are decoding you. Do you have the discernment to understand the signifiers of a luxury holiday? Do you go troppo
in Bali or do you travel to see natural wonders? The second
thing about people who ask *what you do* is that they genu-
inely don't care about you as a person. Because you are not a
person, you are reduced to what you do, and what you do is
an economic question.

Eduardo handed me a beer and asked what kind of writing
I did. I tried to articulate the idea of how a low-selling prose
poem book would legitimise me, but it just came out as chaos.
Eduardo mentioned a popular poem from Latin America and
I just nodded, drawn to the beauty of his black eyes and the
eyelashes that framed them. With all that Kane fucking, I had
forgotten how much I loved deep black eyes. Black eyes contain
all the mysteries of the galaxy. They are magically impenet-
rable, unlike blue eyes, which are often faded and weak.

I wanted to compliment his eyes as he reached over to put
together a plate for me. His low-hanging tank exposed the
whole side of his body, the flank of meat with its defined lat
muscles, and I even got a peek at his brown nipples. I exhaled
a breath, the moisture could have run against his skin. He
kept leaning forwards and reaching, putting different things
on the plate. He turned his head once, to make sure that I
was looking. My eyes ran up and down his arm, looking at
the terrible tattoo on the lovely muscles. I had to stop myself
from running my fingertips along his skin.

You have a lovely tattoo, I said to him. He said that it had meaning, and I wanted to slow clap.

The conversation turned to his job in finance. He liked the office culture, but the work bored him. I looked over to Kane and Aleks again; they were talking closely and had forgotten about us. Eduardo told me he looked forward to the film awards season, when they could spend the day at work discussing the best and worst of the red carpet. We kept talking and drinking; my brain left my body, but no one noticed. Another beer cap popped, and someone said, We truly are in a golden age of television. Fruits were picked at and someone said, We are buying a place in Bowral. Eduardo moved his mouth in my direction, making sure that I was watching as he formed the words. I eye-banged him. His thick lips pushed up and out as he put a plantain between them. When the sun started to set, Kane and Aleks said that they were going off together. They stood up, dusted their clothes and walked away over the grass, between the trees. Me and Eduardo were silent. In the distance we could make out Kane and Aleks in the day's-end light, embracing under a tree.

⊞

It was left to Eduardo and me to pack up the picnic. He folded the blankets in half, rolled them up and put them in tote bags. We put what was left of the food in some of the eskies and dumped empty beer bottles in the bushes. Eduardo held a bunch of bags in each hand and the veins on his arms popped. There were some more bags on the ground, and he looked at them and then at me. I felt embarrassed enough to pick them up. I asked Eduardo if we were going to pick up the eskies; he told me not to worry. Leave them! Just disposable Styrofoam!

It was getting dark and the bushes were casting messy shadows. We walked to the massive wrought-iron gates and stood between the posts, two giant sandstone chess pieces. Eduardo pointed down past Woolloomooloo to show me where he lived. He asked if I wanted to help him take the stuff home. When he said the word home, his lips rounded in an involuntary pout I subconsciously registered as an invitation for a blow job.

We left the gardens and crossed the road, walking over to long metal stairs attached to the side of a small cliff. Each step made a metallic sound as our feet connected. As we descended, I looked down at the expensive apartments on the pier. Eduardo said, Wouldn't it be amazing to live there and wake up to fresh coffee over the water?

Part of me wanted to roll my eyes so hard. Another part of me wanted to wake up in that apartment to the smell of black coffee mixing with the salt air of the harbour.

Beyond the pier was a military ship that huddled against a base. On the other side of the cove, towers rose out of trees in

Potts Point and the skyline was filled with cranes. The cranes were a permanent fixture of the Sydney skyline and I waited for the time when they would be decorated with rainbow flags and Southern Cross symbols.

Eduardo told me how he and Aleks had met. It was two years ago, at a sex party on the Australia Day long weekend. The hosts were a lawyer and a photographer – he enunciated each syllable of their careers but didn't mention their names. Probably because he didn't remember names.

Eduardo got there early and entered the apartment to find both hosts in black fluffy robes. He noticed the leather couches – easy to wipe off Crisco spills or KY lubricant accidents. The rugs had been removed from the floor, leaving bare polished wood.

The lawyer had dirty blond hair and sat on the sofa with his legs spread and an arm resting on the back. Eduardo decided to get to work and kneeled in front of the lawyer. While the photographer went to prepare drinks, he opened the lawyer's robe. He was going down on the host when Aleks walked into the apartment. Eduardo looked up with his mouth full of the lawyer and saw Aleks standing there and realised that they were soulmates. He wanted to say hello, but his mouth was full and his knees on the bare polished floor were rubbed raw.

I said that it sounded like a real blow-job meet-cute. Eduardo gulped air as he told me about bobbing up and down on the lawyer while he watched Aleks undress. He liked the soccer-star definition of Aleks's body; it was refreshing after all the muscle queens and their douche-faggery.

The street narrowed and we walked past a micro-park. This place used to be filled with tranny hookers, said Eduardo. You mean transgender sex workers, I told him. Eduardo said he guessed I would know; after all, most of their clients came from the area where I lived. Men who were married with children but still wanted a chick with a dick. Eduardo told me about all the complaints he made to his body corporate. I told him I thought transgender sex workers were heroes just like the ANZACS. He made a pfft noise. He told me that he had come from poverty and if he hadn't worked so hard in his career he would be the one working corners. He escaped it by believing in himself. The transgender sex workers should do the same. Just believe in themselves.

Eduardo strutted as he described how he'd terraformed the suburb. A sadness fell on me: Sydney's Not in My Back Yarders were a form of government. Whether it was the rich getting rid of sex workers or the rich getting rid of the poor. In Sydney, land is precious, and humans are just speed bumps or the Luxe SUVs that run them over. I changed the subject and asked Eduardo to tell me more about the sex party.

He described the line of muscle that ran in between Aleks's pecs and the way it caught his attention. As he talked about the way Aleks kissed him, his eyes expanded, two big, black whirlpools sucking me in.

It was a pretty average sex party story. Drugs and bodies were consumed. The TV was turned to the music channel and young women's bodies writhed on the screen while the men performed every possible configuration with each other. There was a sixty-nine with a man either side thrusting into the figures fellating each other – a pig on a spit – as the fourth man serviced the nipples and holes he could access. Eduardo described the action in a sports commentator's voice: the photographer had a yogi's flexibility, the lawyer had pelvic thrusting power and Aleks was a good all-rounder with the second biggest cock after Eduardo's. It was a real workout – everyone sweated, muscles engorged, and heart rates soared.

But as Eduardo connected with Aleks on that polished wooden floor, the men reoriented themselves around the obvious chemistry between the new couple. The lawyer and the photographer moved to the periphery, orbiting Eduardo and Aleks as they spent more and more time kissing and licking each other. Eduardo told me this story in the form of a boast, to show his physical prowess and mastery of the erotic arts. But he rounded off the story by reaffirming that they were definitely soulmates. It demonstrated his bravado and his pathos.

I told him that ignoring others was bad group-sex etiquette. Eduardo disagreed. He said that the couple were happy to introduce people who would have good synergy, that the networking and exchange between them would create good outcomes. I raised one eyebrow at the business speak.

Leaving the harbour, we walked deeper into the city. The terrace houses had matte walls and shiny paint on their mouldings; manicured bushes grew out of ceramic planter boxes the same colour as the walls. The cloned residences repeated in different colours until we arrived at the Horizon building, where Eduardo lived. He put down his bags and gestured with an open palm, presenting the tower – he even gave a slight flutter of spirit fingers for theatricality. He asked me to come in, and I followed him towards the entrance; swift curves rising storeys above us arced around the sky. The thuggish geometry of the entrance held the building up.

In the elevator I juggled the bags in my arms. Eduardo told me that Aleks would have gone back to his own place at The Republic. He was talking about another of Sydney's landmark buildings, essentially a series of terrace houses in a modernist box. So, you still live separately? I asked.

Eduardo said that he really liked his place; he preferred high-rise blocks and had a dream of living in the orange and plastic Renzo Piano building. He had tried to convince Aleks that they should sell both their places and move in together. There was a confidence in his voice when he spoke about Aleks; even knowing that Aleks was off with another man, he didn't stutter.

I didn't expect an apartment in a famous tower to be decorated with designer replica furniture, but Eduardo didn't try to hide it. He said he got all his furniture online for a good price. The interior had a monochrome colour scheme, with ecru curtains and rugs coloured in desert sand. There was a black-leather-and-metal Wassily chair and it had started to age from sunlight damage, making it look like a modernist antique. As I surveyed the apartment, I realised that I was coming around to the idea of fakes, that there were ways to make them authentic.

Eduardo dumped his bags in the kitchen, then took the bags from me and just plopped them on the floor. He fixed me a drink I didn't ask for and told me that he was going to have a shower. I went onto the balcony to look over the cityscape, but the curve of the railing swept my gaze into the night sky. When he came out he wore a towel and his skin shone. His stomach was flat, his chest slightly concave, and he beckoned me inside with a finger.

I was ordered to take a shower and clean under my Greek foreskin. He specifically said Greek foreskin, so I said, I'd do anything for your Latin bubble butt. When I came out of the shower, I couldn't find Eduardo. I looked in the kitchen and saw that the booze was left out. In the living room the TV displayed a music channel with young women in heels and bikinis spinning around a pole that disappeared into the galaxy.

I found Eduardo in the bedroom wearing a neon yellow jockstrap. He pushed me onto the bed. I propped myself up with pillows and he did a slutty walk to the stereo and turned it on. He played Bomba Estéreo, their alternative Latin beats creating a soundtrack for him to dance to. I watched as he moved his hips around and around, performing for me alone.

Rubbing his hands over his torso, he shimmied towards the mirrored door of the built-in wardrobe. His palms struck the mirror and he extended his arms out in a starfish, leaving two diagonal streaks on the glass. He turned to look over his shoulder at me, gyrating his hips. His butt cheeks jiggled, and I got instantly hard and started playing with myself. His eyes still on me, he ran his unusually long tongue around his lips and over his chin, leaving a slick saliva shine around his mouth. He turned to the mirror and licked the glass. I moved my hand quicker. His lips connected with his reflection and his eyelids closed slowly, shutting himself off from the world. He kissed his own image, arching his lower back to push out his bubble butt. I moaned loudly and came all over my chest. He turned around and looked at my mess. Lick it up, I said.

17.

After high school I had more time for men. And as my animus increased, my mum's illness escalated. There was a stiffening in myself and a crumbling in my mum.

Away from home I became more of an actual person. A shitty job in retail helped me develop life skills and my body had that early twenties goodness. I tried to blossom into my manhood, using rites of passage or just the passages of men's backsides.

The less Mum went out, the more ill she became. I came home from work one day and found her standing perfectly still in the corner of the room. She had her ear pressed against the wall, and when I walked in she bit her knuckle – the Greek signal for *shut up or there will be trouble*. I didn't ask what she was listening to in the wall.

Once, just as I was about to leave the apartment, I found her standing on a dining chair, reaching up to press the adhesive backs of two plastic hooks onto the wall on either side of the window. She had found an old broom and wrapped a sheet of black plastic around the handle to make a curtain. As I opened the door to leave she called me over to help. I got up on another chair and took one end of the broom handle and we slid it through the plastic hooks. She told me that the new curtains would keep microwaves out of the house. I said that the plastic hooks wouldn't hold.

My mum was stressed at the changes going on around us. At first it was people who made her scared, they were the ones that made her do the bolt. A stranger coming suddenly around a corner or someone standing at the traffic lights could make her shiver. Especially if they turned their head and looked at her. If she saw them twice in a day then she'd go off. Run fast down the street. Then she moved on to objects, thinking that they were being used to communicate things to her. The cross at the top of the church was a sign, telling her that she will be persecuted upon it.

One day she told me that the people working on the new buildings going up in our area were using devices to spy on her. But Mum, ah, those are just Makita drills. She took me onto the balcony and pointed across the street to a surveyor looking through a device on a tripod. I told her that the device wasn't even pointed in our direction and she told me not to be stupid.

There were new developments all around the suburb, and with the new developments came an influx of tradies. The cafes and takeaway shops filled up with people not from the area, ordering egg and bacon rolls. Fewer yeeros were being sold. It made me sad to see the place change and Mum's brain go with it.

One afternoon, I climbed the stairs to our apartment and saw water spreading out from under the door. The carpet squished under my shoes. I opened the door and saw water running down one of the walls in the living room. Mum sat on the sofa rocking back and forth, and I went over to her and kneeled in front of her. She was running her fingers up and down the lace collar of her nightgown. Her eyelids strobed, her gaze darting around the room. She whispered to me that the men were trying to flood her out of the apartment. I told her that it was an accident, a burst water pipe, but I knew she didn't hear me.

I called the representative for the body corporate and they sent over a plumber. He came within thirty minutes and climbed into the ceiling. As soon as Mum saw him she went and hid in the bathroom. I heard him clanging about and then the water slowly stopped. He got out of the ceiling and told me that he would be back with the bill. Mum came out from her hiding place. She said that the water leak was intended to get rid of her, or at least get rid of her evidence. She went to the corner of the room and pulled a newspaper from the bottom of a pile. The soggy paper tore in her hands. She turned to me as it disintegrated in her fingers. She wandered around the room, her shoulders shaking, and said that a key piece of evidence had been destroyed.

I got on my hands and knees and used an old hairdryer on the wet carpet. As each section became dry I moved on to the next one. The process took a few hours. Mum tried to organise all her newspapers. I asked her to turn on the television and she said she didn't want any microwaves going through the house. I asked her if she knew what microwaves were and she told me not to be stupid.

It took the whole night to clean up after the water pipe burst. I didn't want to throw anything away in case it turned Mum up a level. While I hovered over the carpet with the hairdryer, she kept starting to speak, in the middle of a thought – but if the television changes then the electrical storm might stop it? I looked up as she hobbled across the room waving a wet piece of paper. In profile, her nose was a small mountain that ran across the hills of her cheek. I saw her old age and what she would become. I saw myself, a man of fifty with a wrinkled and exhausted face, my beard becoming grey, chasing her through the neighbourhood each time she escaped from the apartment we still shared. I saw myself still stuck out in suburbia and making fleeting arrangements with men at their houses or in public places. More so, I saw what would become of me. Moving her from apartment to apartment. Distracting her with questions: What kinds of flowers do you like? What kinds of plastic flowers are men? I saw myself calming her down when she tapped on the walls, trying to find the electrical devices that had been planted in them.

I spread out my palms to pat down the carpet. I pressed into the parts that were hot from the hairdryer. When I stood up my lower back ached from bending over. Satisfied that the carpet was dry, I went to bed, figuring out a plan.

18.

At the cafe next to Vas Bros Real Estate I sat opposite Basil
and read to him what I had written. My voice was loud and
slow, with a sentimental inflection, pausing at poignant points.
Wogs love a melodramatic arc conveyed through tone; they call
it oral history but it's an excuse to be illiterate. According to
Basil I was a good bullshitter but the writing wasn't working;
he told me to write it like he was writing it. In first person,
you mean? He said yeah, and I told him that if I wrote it that
way I wouldn't be able to put my name on it, that I would
be a ghostwriter. He said that as compensation for my loss of
identity he would up the payment for the book.

Basil wore a tight, shiny grey suit with a pale-blue dress
shirt and silver tie. His shoes were patent-leather brogues, and

the ensemble made him look like a beacon. When he first walked in, I was sitting in the back of the cafe, and once the urge to shield my eyes from his glow had passed I watched how other people responded to him. Older women stole discreet glances and started adjusting their hair, pushing stray strands behind their ears. A young woman in an oversized Original sweat looked at him once then turned away and a smile spread across her face.

As I thought about accepting more money for the book, I held up the long black with my pinkie finger out and put both of my elbows on the table. From outside the cafe came the sound of a helicopter zooming low over the streets, its blades chopping the air, and I assumed that there had been another shooting in the area. The ghetto bird was a familiar sight and sound in Bankstown, a herald that something bad would appear on that night's news. It sounded too close this time, almost skimming the tops of buildings. Basil said that heaps of real estate agents owed him a favour and if the rent on my shithole house in Pemulwuy was too much he could help me find a new place.

Basil took a call on his phone. As he listened to the person at the other end, I wondered how much of me he owned. If he took my writing and passed it off as his own, would that make me any better than a copywriter? Even if Basil did pay for my writing and I couldn't put my name to it, I told myself, it was better than most work. For that brief period when Mum held down the custard powder factory job, I remembered the bags under her eyes when she walked through the door each night. The way she dumped her keys anywhere in the living room before zoning out in front of the television. Her body so tired that she called me to fetch the remote from the other side of the room. Writing Basil's life, in a fake Basil voice, would never be as hard as putting plastic sheeting into machines, or cleaning custard powder vats.

Basil hung up the phone. His brow creased and he looked around the cafe as if only now becoming aware of his surroundings. His breathing was shallow and I asked what was wrong. He said that there was an emergency at one of his buildings, he had to get on site and see if everything was alright. He drank his macchiato in one gulp; as he put the cup down it clashed on the saucer. Outside I heard the sirens of the fire trucks, tearing through the streets, heading into the heart of Bankstown. Basil darted out of the cafe, excusing himself when he bumped into people.

I went to the cashier to pay for the coffees. When I stepped out of the cafe, I saw three black cockatoos sitting in a bottlebrush tree, black feathers against red flowers.

⊞

I had never been the curiosity-killed-the-cat type. But when Basil ran off, and I heard the helicopter and fire trucks, something in me clicked, the sirens hyping up my blood. Old wogs would have called the three black birds a sign.

I followed the sirens, crisscrossing through the streets and back alleys. At a designated pedestrian crossing, cars didn't stop; it was rush hour and getting home was more important than obeying laws.

I walked through the train station foyer to the east side of Bankstown Plaza. Once it had been an actual plaza, a giant, paved expanse with trees. Then they – whoever they are – redeveloped it, putting a road right through the middle. It cut the place in half, dispersing the youth gangs who knifed each other and the seniors doing tai chi. It killed the businesses but the locals never stopped calling it the plaza, even though it was now an intersection.

Down from the plaza, I could see smoke billowing into the sky. Everyday business went on – people passed each other on the pavement and jaywalked across roads, going into delis, Viet marts and bubble tea joints. Only one in every ten people stopped to look at the smoke. They looked up, identified the apartment block it was coming from and started to walk towards it.

On the road outside the apartment block, police had erected barriers. Cars lined up to take a detour, officers in blue directing traffic into the backstreets. Just beyond the barriers, pedestrians were gathering in clumps on the footpath, looking up at the tower and pointing. In the otherwise empty street were two fire trucks; their sirens were turned off, but their red lights were still spinning, their hazard lights blinking. I saw smoke coming from a balcony on the fifth level. It was a thick, black smoke and I walked towards it: the fire trucks, the smoke, the crowd were all pulling me towards them.

One of the cops directing traffic had a girlish face. As I walked past her I watched her communicate non-verbally with the drivers. Men with thick beards looked at her too long. They paused their cars, held on to their steering wheels and looked her up and down. Eventually they obeyed her instructions. Although the traffic was backed up and the cars moved slowly, no one honked their horn – a rarity in a suburb where people used their horns like Morse code. Drivers saw the flashing lights, police barriers and smoke; they understood the terror occurring too close to them, that bodies would be injured.

I joined the people behind the fire trucks. The crowd was a snapshot of the area's demographics: hijabi teens in brightly coloured scarves that fell down to their waists; an Islander mum with back and sleeve tatts, her four kids held in her radius by an invisible tether; old Arab and Greek men having a casual day out but dressed as if for church; white Australians in jorts taking a detour from the shopping centre. Some of the people had their phones held out, pointed up at the smoke.

We all stood there, looking for information, curious about what was going on. We watched the firemen running in and out of the building and talking to the police. People huddled and pointed, commenting on what they could see. The fire engines kept their lights flashing. More and more people came to huddle and watch what was going on. We couldn't see any fire, just the smoke pouring out from one of the balconies. Residents kept on exiting the main doors of the apartment complex, some of them carried as many devices in their hands as possible, some of them still in robes, with nightmasks on their heads. Most of them joined the crowd watching the scene.

The tower was seven storeys high, a bargain-basement hodgepodge of postmodern architecture with no unifying features. It consisted of a stacked series of boxes made from different materials. The ground floor boxes had brown render and silver polyurethane on the outside surface. One section had grey balconies with long visible streaks of water damage. Next to the line of balconies an off-white wall ran up to the top of the building. There were different window sizes everywhere and one side had metal awnings. Blocks on misshapen blocks, balconies that came from nowhere and wrapped around the corner of the building. The tower appeared to be crumbling based on the architectural style alone.

The newly formed crowd pointed at the different parts of the building. Some people hoped that the fire wouldn't spread, some commented on the plastic cladding, hoping that it wouldn't spread to the plastic outside. When people rubber-neck at car accidents or gather at potential human tragedies, underlying it is a horrible idea that unites us all – a controlled horror – that we might see a dead body, the pain inflicted, flesh rendered lifeless.

A familiar Mustang pulled up at the police barricade. Basil jumped out, his grey suit flashing in the sun. I'd got there quicker than he had; he must have had a hard time driving through the blocked streets. He spoke quickly to the policewoman at the barrier, she pointed to the firemen at the front of the building, and he climbed over the divider and ran through the crowd. He spoke to the commander of the firemen and pointed to the building. He was too far away for me to hear him, but he looked frazzled. Several members of the crowd craned their heads, curious about the man in a suit talking to the commander.

Smoke poured out of the balcony in larger clumps. It was a deep, unnatural black and twisted into itself as it rose. Shouting came from inside the building, and the crowd fell quiet. The boys in blue looked up at the balcony and then spoke into their walkie-talkies. The crowd was waiting, listening for more shouting. Then someone on the street gestured to the other side of the apartment block and yelled, There! There! Oh my god! People pointed at the corner of the tower.

The crowd moved to the other side of the building, the smell of fire was in the air. I ran ahead of them and turned the corner, looking up to the apartment where the smoke was pouring out.

Two young women wearing nursing uniforms were standing on a window ledge. They must have climbed out to escape the fire but had nowhere to go. The window was as tall as they were, and they were hanging on to the top of the frame. Both girls had straight, shoulder-length black hair and were in nursing uniforms. They clung to the bricks and looked around, coughing. The crowd yelled up at them and I kept wondering why the sprinklers weren't going off.

⊞

My hands changed a few days after this. I reached for my phone, but when I looked down I didn't see my thick hairy knuckles; in their place were slim, hairless digits, tiny hands, the same hands that held on to the ledge. I shut my eyes, and under the darkness of my lids two bodies fell to the ground.

⊞

I arranged to see Basil again. He said that he would pick me up because he felt bad about the way our last meeting had ended. I was in my bedroom when he beeped his horn. From the window I saw his Mustang parked illegally in the street.

I grabbed my wallet, phone and keys, and ran out of the house. I opened the passenger door but there was a giant gym bag on the seat. Basil told me to put it in the boot, and

I carried it to the back. The boot popped open. Most of the space was taken up by an A1-sized black plastic document holder. I pushed the document holder to the side so the bag wouldn't crush any important papers. Under the document holder was a bolt cutter about a metre long. Its metal head was a matte black and the handle and grip were emergency red. Why would a property developer need a bolt cutter? I quickly shooed the thought out of my head, covered the bolt cutter with the document holder again, put the gym bag in the boot and closed it.

I got into the car next to Basil. He had just seen his personal trainer, and he wore an activewear polo; under his shorts were compression tights. His scent hit me, a body odour of pepper and musk; it stung my nostrils and turned my stomach. He had tried to mask his sweat with a cheap deodorant that smelled too sweet. I shrank into the passenger seat, the smell making my head swell. I looked at his thighs as they pressed down and thickened against the leather seat, the compression tights like gun barrels through the slit in his shorts. My mouth filled with saliva.

As we drove we listened to techno from the late nineties. Basil wasn't enjoying it on an ironic level; he was one of those people who thought music had peaked in his youth and he was the custodian of these late-nineties house melodies. He was reliving his youth by listening to music that was terrible even when it was released.

We drove all the way to Bankstown, because Basil had another meeting after ours. He got a spot right in front of the cafe. We sat outside, opposite Paul Keating Park, overlooking a children's playground with a bouncy floor. Basil went into the cafe to grab us menus and order himself a protein smoothie. He said he loved this place because it made muscle meals – dishes that included sweet potato, broccoli and lean meat protein. He told me that it catered to the local gym bro community. I looked around and saw what he meant: at the other tables were wog muscle bros scraping at plates with cutlery clutched in their fists. Their bright T-shirts resembling plumage, their elbows flapping at their sides, their freshly shorn hair with fades and produkt – spelled with a *k* – made these men the fanciest birds of paradise.

We ordered food and looked over the park. Basil got a muscle meal and I ordered a watermelon and feta salad and a long black. Cafe culture had come to the suburbs, sitting next to the two-dollar shops and fast food chains. It was now possible to get an almond milk latte with a chia pudding and then walk three hundred metres to get a McDonald's sundae.

On the other side of the park was a statue of Sir Joseph Banks, the famous botanist the city of Bankstown was named after. I had seen it up close numerous times. He wore old-timey pantaloons that rode up his crotch, and his jacket had a tail that covered his arse. His face was set in iron, high cheekbones and a perfect nose, his eyes looking up and to the left as if he was lost in thought about how lovely it was to classify and name plants.

I put my phone on the table next to Basil's plate and opened the voice app to record him. What I had seen at the apartment block scarred me, I put my own cladding over my memories of the fire and the two bodies falling.

When our meals came, I asked Basil why he'd been called to the tower fire. He chewed his food and swallowed it; I watched the lump expand his throat, moving his Adam's apple up and down. His cutlery clinked as he put it on the plate. He wiped his mouth with the back of his hand, turned his head to check on his car and then faced me. Behind us the gym bros flapped their elbows as they ate, and a girl came out to serve them more protein shakes.

Five years ago, Basil was part of the conglomerate who had built the place. The cops had called him because they couldn't contact anyone from the strata company that managed it. Basil raised his hand to his collar and pulled out the thin gold cross on the too-thick necklace. He shut his eyes and I saw his thick lashes against his skin; he muttered a little prayer in Greek and put the gold to his lips. His face was slightly flushed from the exercise he had done, or maybe with emotion over the two women who had fallen from the tower. He kissed the cross again and tucked it back under his shirt. He patted it and opened his eyes.

I asked why the sprinklers didn't work in the building. He put his index finger on my phone to stop the voice recorder.

There were no sprinklers in the building, he said. The building was designed to be less than twenty-five metres high. That meant it was below the height at which sprinklers were mandatory. It was a deliberate tactic to cram in as many residential units as possible without incurring the expense of a sprinkler system.

I asked how much below twenty-five metres the building was. He picked up his knife and fork and chopped up broccoli. He said it was thirty centimetres under. He stabbed the broccoli with his fork and his knife scraped against the plate. He lifted the mini green tree to his mouth, looked to the side and stealthily put it into his mouth.

Over the past few days I had kept remembering the girls' hands unclasping the window frame. As soon as I saw the two bodies falling through the air I had turned my head so I wouldn't see how they landed. I had to put a cordon sanitaire in my mind, so I could continue doing my job.

As Basil chewed, looking down at his plate, I asked him what his legacy would be. Basil used his fork to point to the other side of the park. He asked if I could see the statue of Sir Joseph Banks. That cunt – what was he? A botanist? Whole fuckin' burb named after him. He was a nerd gronk, wore weird pants and picked up plants. Plants! Boring! He named shit that already had names. Gossip was that he took the head of Pemulwuy the resistor and sent it to England. And they still put up a statue of the guy! We celebrate him! You wanna know about legacy? It's this: If you suit someone else's story, then they'll build statues of you and name a whole fucking city after you.

Basil kept scraping his plate with his cutlery and turning around to check on his car. Behind him in the park a group of schoolboys had gathered with a football. Half of the boys took off their shirts. I spent the rest of our meeting watching them over his shoulder. After playfully throwing the ball around, they began a game of touch football and then started tackling each other. Soon a fight broke out. I looked closer but couldn't see who was fighting whom. Was it the skins or the shirts that were winning? Limbs everywhere. Fists landing blows reminded me of flesh hitting concrete.

19.

Having another interview with Kamilla was an excuse to see her again. In the previous interview most of her answers were about her time at the salon or her current work with Basil. Her boss bitch nonsense was peppered with grooming and skin-care tips. Don't be scared to use a tinted moisturiser! Always pluck your eyebrows from underneath! Silica can strengthen your nails too!

I pulled out my phone and opened the voice recorder. We were sitting on the couch and she pulled out a Swarovski cigarette holder. The slim silver box had a pattern of crystals on one side. The tiny crystals were brown, beige and white – a sad hetero rainbow. She brought her fingernail up to her lips. Shh! A secret – occasionally she had a cigarette. I would be murdered if I told Basil. Occasionally is okay, I said. Everyone has secrets.

Kamilla told me that she was busy with organising Basil's diary. She was too busy for secrets. Her eyes flicked to mine, and the tone of the room shifted. I'd thought we had a good rapport, but I now saw she was suss on me, especially since I knew that there might have been a bruise under that makeup.

Her claws opened the case; inside were six white cigarettes with gold tips. I took one in my fingers and Kamilla got up to find a lighter.

If I played the glamour-struck dippy fag, she wouldn't see me as a threat. I followed her to the sliding door. She pulled it open and the noise of traffic punched into the apartment: angry horns, grunts of revving cars and hydraulic buses hissing. Outside, she folded her arms and leaned on the balcony railing, lighting her cigarette with a cheap disposable lighter. I took it in my hand, flicked the Bic and asked her if she wanted to tell me anything about Basil off the record.

She exhaled and the smoke blew across her face. The cigarette was held low between her knuckles, the tips of her nails two beacons for the glowing stick. Kamilla told me she organised his spending. I am integral to his operation! I believed her words, the authority with which she delivered her script.

A silence fell between us, filled with the sounds of traffic. Every time I looked at her face I noticed the thick sheen of makeup. I tried again to find traces of the bruise under the foundation.

She pointed towards the clump of towers on the Bankstown horizon, in the area zoned for business. In the centre of them was a crane; Kamilla said it was called a luffing crane. She liked to say that word: luffing. The lilt of the first letter, the muted neutrality of the first syllable and the rolling *ing*. L-uff-ing, she repeated. It was a kind of crane built for jobs that were in the middle of tall buildings. At night the arm of the luffing crane would be raised high and the brakes turned off, so the operator's cab and the arm could move around in the wind; this would prevent the crane from being blown over.

You know what? she said. Sometimes I lie in bed and imagine cranes just spinning around at night as the wind blows.

Our cigarettes finished, I followed her back inside. I watched the back of her head and that long hair. She said she needed to be excused. I took my place on the couch. I was intrigued by the work Kamilla did and by the way her brain worked. She was obsessed with the fine details of schedules and shades of foundation on skin, yet there was also a part of her that thought about cranes alone at night, spinning around in a suburban wind.

The laptop in front of me was open. I pressed on one of the keys and it awoke: the screen flashed white and filled with the perfect boxes of a digital calendar. Basil's meetings were carefully noted in each box, colour-coded in blue and green. I was envious of the precision and order of his life. There were even scheduled appointments with a personal trainer.

I ran my eyes across the next few days in his calendar. Meetings with council and finance companies, site inspections, all routine. But two entries were shaded in red. The second was typed in capital letters and set in inverted commas: 'POTENTIAL SITE INSPECTION'. The entry above it, also shaded red, just said, 'Pick up stuff', and the location was Keating's Storage World.

Someone like Basil going to a storage place, picking up goods for work, I knew that it was wrong. I wanted to make a note of it. I opened my wallet to find an old receipt to write down the info but there was no pen around. I pulled out my phone and used the camera to take a picture. The phone made a click sound that echoed in the apartment. I heard the toilet flush. The laptop was still lit up, so I pushed the screen down and hoped she wouldn't notice.

Kamilla entered the living space and told me she heard the camera. I told her that I was taking a selfie and she accepted it. I've got a pretty picture of me! I said to her and she suggested that I could go shopping with her when the book comes out, to find something to wear to the launch.

20.

I would get the halal snack pack myself.

As I typed sentences on my laptop, changing the epic Basil story into first person, I could hear young boys yelling outside in the street. Fuck ya gronk, and Sick one, bro. I heard the whizz of skateboard wheels and then a teenager's voice yelled out, You dumb poofta. Immediately I stood up and paranoia rose in me. Somehow, they must have discovered that there were gays with jobs and French bulldogs living among them. Had they seen me and Kane buying groceries? Fear flooded my faculties, and my mind skipped to a future where I shook in the foetal position on the living room floor while eggs were thrown at our front door, the yolk running down the handle.

Then the yells overlapped into playfulness and I realised that the street urchins were expressing a casual homophobia directed at each other. I was safe. My stomach growled, hunger replacing my fear, my mind came back to my body, my body was back in the room, and I thought about getting a kebab for breakfast.

Kane came to stand on the other side of my bedroom door and told me he needed to go out, he needed to eat bad food. Glory! We had finally synced! Kane confessed he needed a mouth party because of the terrible sex he'd had with some strangers last night. I told him that I was planning on getting a halal snack pack anyway.

Because of my weird writing hours I often lost track of the days, but I thought it must be the weekend because of the BMXlings yelling outside. Kane said, Red red ready or not, and came through the door jingling coins in his hand and wearing a white singlet with New Balance emblazoned on it. I was wearing black activewear that made me invisible and we went to the shops.

On the steeple above the main entry to the shopping centre was a sign saying PEMULWUY MARKETPLACE, with an eight-pointed star above the words. Next to the entry was a Gloria Jean's coffee shop. Four young girls were sitting at an outside table drinking Crème Brûlée Chillers with whipped cream and blue sprinkles on top, their moistened lips puckered around thin straws. Their T-shirts said *Je t'aime* and *Girl* in a cursive font. One of the girls with a braid on the side of her head bum puffed the smoke, holding the cigarette too low between her fingers. I almost laughed at how phoney she looked, but then she noticed me and Kane walking together. She tilted her head to the side and focused her eyes to read us. She must have assumed we were a couple. She mouthed, Cute, nudged her friends and pointed at us. Just then a long train of trolleys stacked together rolled past, pushed by a man in a hi-vis vest.

As we walked through the shopping centre, Kane swayed and leaned against my arm in a melancholy way. I thought he was going to tell me about a recent heartbreak, but he mentioned again his fear of property prices dropping. He made a sad, vulnerable face as he thought out loud about the mosque and how it would depreciate his assets. His voice shook, and his eyes welled. I wanted to put my hand on his shoulder to console him.

A boy in his mid-twenties wearing a green polo shirt approached us. He had shoulder-length blond hair with a centre part and held a hopeful clipboard in his hand. He spoke to us in a gap-year British accent and wanted to tell us about fundraising for the wilderness. When Kane waved him away the boy looked briefly distressed. He shook it off and perked up, and we watched him approach a young family of Hazara refugees. His opening line to them: Are you interested in saving endangered animals?

Kane took out his wallet, put a twenty-dollar bill in my hand and told me I knew his order. I walked up to the Fully Tabooly Kebab Stop. The freshly sliced vegetables sat behind glass in silver trays. Chicken, lamb and beef rotated on metal poles. A man with a beard stood behind the counter. His apron had grease stains where he wiped his hands. Above him were iconic photographs of the food they sold, backlit with white fluorescents. He spoke to me in Arabic and I said, Salam, and ordered a kebab and a halal snack pack in English.

When I paid for the food, he spoke to me in Arabic again and I nodded, pretending I understood. This had happened to me a few times, people speaking to me in their language, like the Turks when I was in Auburn. I liked being mistaken for someone from another culture, not because it made me more interesting, but because I could be someone else. When people projected another culture onto me it made me anonymous, someone other than Pano. Someone who wasn't raised in a messy apartment with a mother who thought a picture of Anthony Quinn as Zorba the Greek was my father.

When I turned around with the food in my hand, still smiling, I saw that Kane was watching.

21.

Somewhere in the Western Suburbs is a sexual health clinic. The grey building has a series of windows that are painted over so people can't see inside. Men enter from a discreet side entrance with a rainbow flag on the door. They keep their hoodies on as they blow in off the street; a crisp southerly wind has carried them all the way from their closets.

I went there once and sat on a plastic waiting-room chair. At first I tapped my fingers on the pink and grey armrests and looked around at the men, trying to make aesthetic judgements on potential trade. But it was hard to make out their bodies through the hoodies, baseball caps and sunglasses, so instead I read the *Pink Triangle Times* – a free newspaper for the LGBTQI community. I opened to a full page of hot headless torsos and next to it were some advertisements selling luxe apartments. It reminded me of Basil. Nerves filled me about writing Basil's story, I opened a doc on my phone and read over the changes I had made, until the nurse called me in. I got up to the part in Basil's childhood where he decided he would dedicate his life to property.

⊞

On the day it was Kane's turn to cook he went to the clinic to get some tests done. In the waiting room, he found a Middle Eastern fish recipe in *Australian Life!* magazine. That night he pan-fried salmon while we discussed the pros and cons of meal plans. Pros: All meals prepared. Cons: Get bored easily. I asked about his day, and he told me about the hooded men in the clinic who were closeted enough to be in Narnia. Tell me about it! Amirite? Kane flipped the salmon with the tongs. The oil sizzled the fish, a million little yellow bubbles scorching pink flesh to white.

When the conversation hit a lull, I brought up the previous day's kebab shop encounter. I told Kane that I liked being mistaken for another race. It showed us how dumb we were when we tried to place people. Told him, that it also made me elated to escape my childhood, pretend to be someone else.

Kane stood tall in front of the integrated rangehood, his spine in perfect neutral, his shoulders down, ignoring what I was saying. The sizzling bubbles of oil fried up some memories. I tried hinting at my upbringing, you know my mum said that the metals in the fish were communicating that . . . Kane changed the topic. No! Loser! Talk! Past is PAST!

This is a great life, Kane explained as he put stalks of asparagus under the grill. I looked over his body and the empty white plates on the dinner table and agreed. This might go away if the mosque gets built, said Kane.

I didn't know exactly what he meant – was he saying that our little gay domestication with its chemical-induced coupling and curated food portions would disappear? When he pulled out the stalks of asparagus they were burnt green twigs. Annihilation hung over our dinner as he poured a tahini sauce over the fish. Thin yellow sauce pooled on each plate. I asked if the sauce made this dish Middle Eastern and he nodded.

⊞

The next night it was my turn to cook. When I told Kane I was making chicken and vegetables in a Mediterranean style he asked if my mum cooked a lot. I didn't want to continue the loser talk, so I asked if he could blend tomatoes in the NutriBullet for a sauce. As I prepared the meal he hovered in the kitchen. He wiped away the juice I spilled cutting lemons and pulled out the handheld Dyson to vacuum up stray oregano leaves. I fried the chicken legs in coconut oil and when they were done I covered them with a lemon oregano mix to mask the nutty taste of the oil. In the pot I steamed two servings of okra.

I transferred the food to an Art Nouveau oval tureen and put it in the middle of the laminate table. I poured water from a replica Marc Newson jug into highball glasses. The table was set, and the chicken and okra were in the tureen. Flat white plates sat on colourful ethnic placemats. The dishes contrasted with the fake wood grain of the table, and I told Kane that I didn't want to lose this place.

Kane said that if I pretended to be Muslim, I could be a voice against the mosque and he wouldn't have to sell up, to avoid losing value on the house.

Wouldn't you want to do it for this place? For the thing we have here? For Frenchie, the French bulldog? You know how Muslims feel about dogs, it's haram or hara or something. We might as well of called him Charlie Hebdo. And what about the children? We all share the dream! How would those poor kids that are just coming out in high school feel about having some big homophobic, K9-hating, cartoon-killing religion down the street? Cartoons mate? Why would you hate Garfield? The campaign with Wally didn't work. He's gone! Lorna's trying her best, but she's fresh out of ideas. We need you, mate! It's the only way to stop the rezoning: a gay Muslim? Against the mosque? Those pink-dollar poofs would come out in force. Angry dildos and all. No one could say anything.

Me and Kane had started having sex again; we reanimated it one night when I was brushing my teeth in the bathroom and he came up behind me and flicked the waistband of my underwear. It was that easy, just the slapping sound of elastic on my skin. Our regular couplings were comfortable enough for a brief release, the cuddling was a simulacrum of authentic affection, and it meant we wouldn't have to go through the embarrassment of sending nude photos of ourselves to strangers online.

I'll do it, I said, sitting at the table. I looked at Kane and said that I would pretend to be someone else. Kane looked down at his phone and SMSed Lorna for a meet.

I served the food onto Kane's plate first. He was engrossed in his phone so I started eating, cutting through the flesh of my drumstick with my knife. Eventually I got sick of using cutlery. There's an old Greek saying: Women and chicken, you gotta use your hands. I put down the knife and fork, ripped the drumstick off the thigh and bit into it. My teeth tore at the flesh around the bones. When I had stripped all the meat, I nibbled at the cartilage of the joints, and when that was gone I cracked the bones and slurped out the marrow and realised that I was living my best life.

22.

Lorna suggested we meet on the streets of Pemulwuy. She liked to walk and organise things; it reminded her of a standing desk with a treadmill. She wore camo-patterned activewear and pushed the pram back and forth with one hand, holding a phone to her ear with the other. She was speaking in a corporate register, her voice low and well-modulated, her vowels rounded. From what I could hear she was brokering a meeting between the gay Albanian Muslim who feared the mosque and any reporter who would listen. I tapped her on the shoulder and she put up one finger, asking me to wait until she was finished.

During our walk and talk, Lorna had told me that she was having some difficulty finding mainstream traction for the story. All her old contacts had moved on. They were in advertising now, because money was our real fourth estate. News editors and special-interest journalists from mainstream papers kept hanging up on her. She had even tried contacting entertainment reporters, but a story about homosexuality and religion was of no interest to them unless it was about a fashion designer saying something anti-Semitic or a fall line of Cordoban-influenced kaftans. But she kept ploughing away because she missed the work.

As she spoke on the phone, Lorna shook the pram with one hand. When her baby started to whimper, she took longer power-strides with her battering pram. She looked back at me, frowning, her eyes turning into two little slits, wordlessly instructing me to follow. I obeyed. Each house in the street lined up perfectly with the next. Fences on one side matched fences on the other. On one house a Juliet window might have a green balconette, on the other it might be dark green. If one house was painted coral pink with taupe accents, the next was pewter with salmon pink accents. Pemulwuy was a physical representation of the new car smell.

Lorna veered off the footpath and onto the smooth new tar of the road, still talking. There were no potholes, no bumps – not that it would have mattered: her space-age pram had the best suspension.

When she had finished the conversation, she held the phone away from her face and hung up. She placed it in a zip pocket in the sleeve of her panelled shirt. Her baby started crying and Lorna squinted at the child. The corners of her mouth turned up; she cooed at the baby.

Lorna was someone who applied the same rigour to raising her new baby as she once had to her job – poring over books and websites to research optimal sleep patterns, scheduling boob-milk pumping and baby yoga classes. She would raise her child with precise contemporary ideas informed by the neuroscience on emerging minds and effective behavioural techniques for mammals. From its inception the child had advantages I'd never had. But I wasn't green with jealousy or red with resentment. Rather, when Lorna spoke to me I reflexively stepped back and tensed my muscles, knowing that Lorna herself, and her child – when it grew up and encountered people like me – would also take a step back, observe me from a distance. They would instinctively know that I hadn't been raised to a plan, book or ideology. They would see the deficit in me and treat me with a resigned compassion.

I trailed behind her, looking at how the kerb blended into the street in a smooth angle. I had come far from where I grew up – an apartment complex where children pointed at a nature strip and asked their parents if they could play in the park.

Lorna told me that an interview and a photo shoot had been organised for the following day. I must have looked alarmed, because she patted my shoulder and told me to relax. She said the character I was becoming didn't need to give his name to the journalist. The character had to hide his identity out of fear of reprisals from his own community. His need for anonymity would add mystery and fear, making the story more urgent while appealing to anti-Muslim biases. The photo would be taken from behind. For example, I might be sitting on a park bench looking over a lake – a regular stock photo about depression.

⊞

In the morning the work wasn't coming to me. I sat in front of lined yellow pads holding a pen, a coffee cup burning my hand. I tried making the prose poems – short blocks representing the uniquely suburban experience – come, but I was bulwarked by writer's block so I thought that I'd rather go for a drive. I SMSed Kane asking if I could take his car out for a joyride. He replied five minutes later: Ye but fil her up.

Lorna had sent me a reminder that my photo shoot for the fag rags was this afternoon. I SMSed back asking if the photographer was hot and if I should let a nipple slip. She replied using all capital letters and exclamation marks to tell me he was STRAIGHT!!!

Inside the car I gently touched the button for the windows and they shot up, barriers closing me off from the outside. The air conditioning blasted my face. I connected my phone to the speaker system via Bluetooth and put on a vaporwave banger. When that genre first emerged I wasn't keen, but the rolling synths and rising arpeggios made it a perfect soundtrack for driving through suburbia.

As I drove along a road just outside Pemulwuy, I looked at people waiting in line at a bus stop with a clear perspex shelter. An old woman with an empty shopping trolley was sitting on the bench with her handbag beside her. A group of school students stood behind the shelter. Their regulation polo shirts were untucked but buttoned right up to the neck. One of the boys was smoking a cigarette. As the traffic slowed for a red light, the cigarette teen glanced at me in the car. We exchanged a look: I admired the way he made the uniform his own thing and he looked at me in air-con comfort with a green glint in his eye.

The wide suburban roads were good to drive on, but constantly stopping at traffic lights wrecked the flow I was getting into. I wanted to pair the speed of the car with the tempo of the music. After snaking through the suburbs, I ended up on the M4. Parts of the two-lane motorway were being turned into three lanes. I caught glimpses of what was going on behind the temporary fences – workmen clearing a strip of grass and trees, others jackhammering into the road. Signs apologised for the inconvenience but told us it was necessary to expand the motorway to exemplify future benefit to New South Wales. Bright yellow government signage imposing the Judeo-Christian morality of suffering in the present to gain a long-term benefit.

I moved to the left-hand lane. Women in hi-vis gear held signs telling people to slow down. Some of the women had grey strands in the ponytails emerging from beneath their orange hard hats. Younger women had neat plaits falling all the way down their back. One woman looked to be around my age. She had a short, bobbed haircut that was dyed red, red as an alarm. She waved at me as I passed, and her fingernails were stop sign bright.

I kept driving against the fences, slowing down when the signs told me, speeding up when I could. The motorway curved, rose and descended. It was true what they said about driving in Sydney, that it was interesting because of the haphazard way the place was put together. There were no straight lines, no roads that didn't dip and rise. And all around me I could see cranes. Rising above an empty lot that looked like a football field of rubbish. Standing erect next to a block of shiny new apartment buildings, the intricate cross-weaving of the base rising to the operator box.

This was Sydney's new world order: cranes everywhere and women in hi-vis telling us to slow down. A constant flurry of something being built, something being torn down, while unseen forces made fortunes. New roads as shiny as the mirrored high-rise apartments, while little old ladies waited at bus stops.

Leaving the M4, I veered into a McDonald's and parked the car. I ordered a thickshake and sat in a booth to write notes on a napkin. I wrote down the things I saw, cranes, roads, bus stops, development, cars, green nails. The plastic straw scraped the roof of my mouth. I twisted my face in pain. There were no other customers in the McDonald's, no one saw my embarrassment. I took my notes and left. I needed to go home and prepare for the photo shoot.

As I drove back through Pemulwuy, I looked at the symmetrical streets, the clean front yards and oh! the order of the place. The car almost parked itself; it knew where to go. When I entered the house the neutral, muted colours of the carpet and the furniture created a comfort in me, a release from the tension of driving on curved motorways surrounded by garbage fields that grew cranes.

Walking through the house, somewhere in the back of my mind I had a blind date with the photographer. I took a quick shower, sprayed a perfume called Wanting on my body and heard a knock on the door. I got dressed quickly and opened the door holding the towel in my hand. The photographer's clothes were black, faded almost to grey. His T-shirt was lighter than his jeans, and he wore a vest with multiple pockets. A boxy camera bag hung over his shoulder.

We introduced ourselves. His name was Mehmet, and he told me to call him Mem. He was a friend of Lorna's. She had briefed him on what was needed and sent him the location of where she wanted the photo taken. It was going to be at the lot where the mosque was going to be built.

I wore a singlet and felt the cool change roll over my shoulders. Mem had thick chestnut hair to his shoulders. He was one of those light-coloured Ottomans. We walked side by side, matching each other's steps. Mem said that he grew up in the ghetto suburbs around here and he remembered when this place was a brickworks. These too-clean streets and too-neat houses were anathema to him. I told him that these too-clean streets and too-neat houses were the reason I moved in. I play-flirted with him, something most progressive straight men will tolerate because they think they're being edgy. Winking at him, I said that we were natural enemies because of the whole six hundred years of occupation. He said he wasn't raised that way, because his dad was one of those Turkish communists.

Then he said that he didn't know much about the Albanian community anyway. I stumbled and my arms dropped. I had already forgotten that I was supposed to be an Albanian. I swallowed hard and said that I didn't really want to talk about my community.

The empty lot where we were going to take the photograph was at the end of a row of houses. A chain-link fence surrounded the scrubby, overgrown plot. Littered in the grass were soft drink bottles and beer cans. A magpie warbled just as a passing car slowed to see what we were doing. Mem put down his bag and took out his camera. He took off one lens and swapped it for a wider and shorter one. He said he wanted to take some test shots and I reminded him the photos couldn't show my face. I turned my back, put my fingers through the chain metal and shook it, rattling the fence. I kept shaking the chain-link fence and behind me the camera clicked away. You look like you're in jail, said Mem. Amid the fun of the play-acting I turned around and looked right into the lens as the camera clicked. I held up my hand and told Mem not to use that photo. It wouldn't do any good for me to be exposed.

23.

I walked through Newtown station, ready for my first inter-view as someone else. The open plaza station design had a try-hard continental feel. There were murals on the walls referencing the Indigenous and colonial history of the place. The white men in the murals looked Ye Olde Worlde with their grandad collars and long beards. Walking past the mural were young men who also had long beards and wore grandad collars.

Further down the street I passed the Greek church. It was so out of place in Newtown. Up and down King Street, old butcheries had been turned into micro bars and takeaway shops turned into sourdough bakeries. The faded pink and cream on the church's facade reminded me of the colours my mother used to wear. The concrete walls and columns as big as trees were supposed to look stoic but they just looked lonely.

On the way to the cafe I bumped into an old university acquaintance. I'd paused at the door of a tanning salon to look at the serious signage displaying the price of a spray tan. I stood there looking at the text in golden Times New Roman, thinking about how a classy font can add dignity even to fake tans. I felt a tap tap tap on my shoulder. I turned around and the university acquaintance said, You! From another life! Are you the Pano that pulled bongs just outside the heritage classrooms?

We'd lost touch when I dropped out halfway through my degree and he was happy to see that I still had a heartbeat. I said, Sorry I never called you, but I got another low-paying job and the police were cracking down on the marijuana growers in Goulburn, which meant I paid thirty dollars for a twenty.

He asked what I was doing in his area. I didn't want to say that I had a meeting with a journalist where I was going to pretend to be a Muslim. We stood in silence for a moment, and then I told him I was on my way to a date. He asked what I was up to. That question was a way of figuring out my status – if I was worthy of a slow-drip cold coffee date in the future. I told him I was writing a character interrogation of aspirational diasporic communities. It sounded much nicer than saying that a property developer was paying me to do a vanity project. That's amazing, he said. I told him it was no big deal. He said, Right on, bro! Listen to your chakra. I told him I was late for my date and walked off.

I noticed a man with blond dreadlocks skipping barefoot past the giant mural of the Aboriginal flag with a picture of Martin Luther King on it. My hands kept trying to find a place for themselves. I walked past a beggar in front of a supermarket. College boys who must have wandered down from the university dropped coins into her cup. I noticed the creative types in clashing outfits who wanted to show the world they were artists. I thought that wearing a nondescript shirt and jeans would have made me invisible, but somehow it made me feel like I stuck out more.

I walked to the cafe with my arms crossed, shrinking into myself. I rehearsed key phrases in my head that Lorna and Kane had workshopped with me. I was going to use the terms 'off the record' and 'on the record'. Off the record I was scared for my life, on the record I didn't think the mosque would be a good fit for a multicultural and tolerant community. I would tell a story about being kicked out of my Albanian family, because, well, gay. My eyes would slightly well up and I would say that I loved my family and community, but we had that post-Yugo Balkan genocidal trauma – it made us crazed. As I was about to cross the road, I realised I was rehearsing my talk out loud and people were looking at me.

The cafe had a limp rainbow flag hanging from a pole outside. I sat on one of the orange chairs inside. The waiter came to me and I ordered a soy latte. He looked at me like I was wearing brown shoes in a black-shoe season, so I asked for an almond latte and he indicated to me that it was acceptable. I looked out towards the street; gay couples walked past arm in arm and I wondered if I would ever know the touch of a lover in a public place. Living gay in the Western Suburbs, meant that public affection was a gamble.

A man sat down opposite me and introduced himself as the journalist. He called himself Cliff and said that he was the longest-serving journalist at the *Pink Triangle Times*. He assumed I was the subject of the interview because of my neatly trimmed beard and out-of-context outfit. Cliff wore a flannel shirt and black Levi's 501s that were so faded they were grey. The classic hack-journo aesthetic crossed the lines of sexuality. As he introduced himself all I could find were his faults. His eyebrows were thin, but they hadn't been trimmed. The skin on his face was blotchy and it seemed like he had never heard of pore refiner. He took out a notepad from his messenger bag and a pen from his shirt pocket.

The waiter put my latte down on the table. He arranged the sugar satchels in a glass and Cliff looked up at him and said, Hi. The waiter asked if he wanted his regular and Cliff looked at me and said that he was a bit of a slut, he took all his interviewees to this cafe. His wink almost made me retch.

Kane had told me to build a rapport with the journalist, so I told Cliff I really liked his article in the *Pink Triangle*

Times on 'How to Renovate Your Sex Dungeon for that Army Barracks Experience'. Cliff was impressed and began the interview by trying to negotiate my name out of me. I told him that I wanted to remain anonymous because I didn't want the article to reach my Albanian family members.

Cliff looked at me suspiciously, and I told him I feared a jihad on my head. Cliff asked if I meant fatwa, and I said, Yeah, I just forgot the name of a thing my religion does, the religion that I was a part of. Cliff said that he thought Albanian Muslims weren't that militant and didn't tend to put fatwas on people and I picked up my latte and slurped on it.

One of the tactics I had been instructed to deploy was flirtation. Create a personal connection by complimenting him and then use a physical connection. I touched the flannel fabric of his shirt and our eyes met. I said that he would understand my need for discretion and, oh, how I loved older men for their wisdom. Bile stirred in my stomach.

From my seat I could see every person coming through the door. My old university friend came in. He looked over at me and turned his hands into a gun and shot at me. I was worried about what he might say, because I once taught him how to make an apple bong. He walked right up to us and before he could say anything I asked if I could talk to him over there. I pointed to the corner.

I took him aside and said, Hey, I don't think it would be a good idea for us to sit together. I told him that I wasn't ready to introduce anyone to my sugar daddy. My old university friend looked at Cliff's ratty clothes. How do you think he keeps his millions! He doesn't spend it on clothes!

When I got back to Cliff, he had this confused look on his face and I turned on the lashes and mouthed, Old fuck. Cliff touched his nose and continued with the interview, asking me about my Muslim community and my fears associated with the new mosque.

At the end of the interview Cliff said that he had something to show me. He pulled out a laptop from his messenger bag and opened it, then turned the screen to face me. I was looking at a photo of the back of my head. The photo had a subaltern masculinity, my freshly shaved hairline giving the appearance of rough trade. Beyond the silhouette of my head was a chain-link fence. The grey metal popped against the blue background.

I wondered about how many men had watched me from this angle the way the camera had, if that constant gaze had affected me in any way.

24.

Visiting my mum in my twenties, she told me about the way men driving past in cars were trying to signal her. It wasn't through their headlights or horns; she claimed that their wheels were irradiating her with beams of energy, in the service of making her confused. Another time I visited, I came to the apartment and found the whole place shut from the light. She was sneaking around, peering between the blinds in windows, opening the door to put her eye against the crack. She told me that she was trying to see if the men were following her. I decided it was time for treatment.

For about six months in my early twenties I danced on podiums in gay nightclubs and it had to stop so I could wake up early and spend days on the phone, trying to get Mum into treatment. Over the phone I pleaded for rescue to assistant nurses and receptionists on rotating shifts. They asked me to call back at certain times and then never picked up the phone again. I often sat next to the phone, holding the receiver between my shoulder and ear. I wrote stuff down as I spoke to volunteers on mental health hotlines. What are her behaviours? they asked. They would ask if I thought she was at risk of self-harm. The only physical symptom I could describe was that her fringe was cut at an angle, which made it hard to look at her if you had a personality type that required symmetry. I described the oversized red T-shirts that had faded to pink worn as dresses. The carpet in the apartment still smelled skanky from the flood, and it filled my nostrils as I begged for help.

I found myself telling these strangers things about my mum I had never told anyone. How when I was a kid she would mistake me for a man trying to get her. She never explained what they would do if they got her. I thought that they had already got her in a way. How she used to do the random bolt when we walked in the street together. Fear becoming small circles and growing into uncontrollable vortexes. All the unaccounted time when I didn't know where she was. How it started with the men she knew, bosses or landlords, and then expanded so that random strangers walking past were in on it too. A man with a walking stick giving a playful wink was someone trying to get her. And then how it increased with

166

devices or objects. Apparently, cars had technology built into their tyres to blast her with radiation. A young pedestrian talking on his mobile was reporting to his superiors what she was doing. As I confessed her symptoms to the phone, the voice on the other end had a name for what was going on but didn't want to pre-empt the diagnosis. She recommended a public clinic near our house.

On a map, I saw that the clinic was next to the hospital. I ran my finger along the streets between Mum's apartment and the clinic. It was a twenty-minute walk. I told Mum that I was taking my nightly contemplative and went to scope the place out.

I walked through the suburbs, taking backstreets and crossing the oval. After walking down a long main road full of cars with violent high beams, I arrived at the hospital.

At the main hospital's reception desk, I asked how to get to the clinic. Even with directions, the place was hard to find, on the edge of the hospital grounds, the entrance concealed behind a bus shelter. Set in a discreet brick wall, two heavy doors led to a waiting room with grey plastic seating and pamphlets about mental health in numerous languages; this was the only reading material. A reception desk protruded from the back wall, with a perspex shield to protect the person inside. The shield had marks, dents and cracks where people had tried to punch through. There were lots of people sitting and standing, waiting for their name to be called out. But the biggest obstacle would be getting her there in the first place.

I sat in the reception area for about five minutes, and watched the nurse behind the perspex barrier. She was exhausted and sarcastic. Her hair was in cornrows and she wiped her nostrils with her broad hand. She let the phone ring out while she typed away one finger at a time on the keyboard.

⊞

The next day I gave Mum the telephone number of the clinic and told her I wanted her to see a psychiatrist. Lying to get her there, I said that the doctors in the clinic worked all-natural, that they treated the health of the soul. She called the clinic and was put through to a doctor. She asked a few questions. When he started to explain what the clinic did, she hung up on him. From under the telephone, in a drawer, she took out a small notebook and wrote down the name of the doctor she'd spoken to. He was on the list of men.

Mum believed there were a vast number of people targeting her. All of these people were men. I pointed this out to her once and she said that women didn't get involved with those kinds of things. She described those kinds of things as men chasing women and making them scared. Chasing women – the way she said it, like it was a game for boys. Although there was a degree of truth to this, her synapses had fizzled and distorted the outside world, making all men a constant threat. Part of me wanted to know what happened, what burned her brain out, but I also wanted to protect my own brain from understanding Mum's experiences.

⊞

A few streets away from our apartment was a house that had a terrible hold over my mother. Every week after late night shopping I remember carrying the plastic shopping bags, trailing behind my mum. When she came to this house she always stopped and turned to look at it. One time she stopped in front of it, dropped her plastic bags and stood completely still until she raised one arm out towards it, her fingers quivering.

The outside light was on, illuminating a tiled veranda with a white balustrade, two columns either side of the door. I gently put the shopping bags down on the pavement and put my hand on Mum's shoulder. I asked what was wrong. She said that a woman was killed by her husband in there. I asked her when it happened. She didn't remember exactly but it was when she first moved into the suburb. It made all the local Greek papers. Her hands covered her face and her head swayed, her chest shuddered.

I could almost understand why she thought men were targeting her. Her whole life, men had been obstacles to her story. Whether landlords or debt collectors or bosses. She lived in a world where men had dominion. To get a job she was interviewed by men and then her tasks were micromanaged by them. All the heads of the Greek community were men and they were the ones that decided the terms of acceptance, the ways in which someone like her, with her no-husband life and offcut fringe could participate.

When my mother developed industrial asthma from cleaning the vats at the custard powder factory, she asked her boss if she could be transferred to another role so she could continue to work. He refused; she ended up leaving and never going back.

I was at home one day when The Boss from Custardo Worx Inc dropped by to check on her. We were watching daytime TV and I was getting a glass of water. There were three polite taps on the door, *knock, knock, knock*, she looked at me confused and asked in a sing-song voice, Who is it? The boss answered his name. It's Dimos. She said she didn't know any Dimos and he said in a gruff voice that it was Dimos her boss. On the television, the audience was shouting Je-rry! Je-rry! Je-rry! She looked at me, put her index finger over her lips to indicate that I should be quiet. Dimos yelled through the door, told her to open up, that they had unfinished business. He hit the door three times, *thud, thud, thud*. Mum gestured frantically, that I should sit on the couch. I took my glass of water over there and she covered me in a blanket, all the way up to my neck. The knocks at the door became stronger, until she relented and opened it. She took steps back from the entrance and Dimos the Boss walked into the house, stalking her. He stopped when he saw me on the couch. He had grey eyebrows and a bald head. I could see the thick clumps of hair coming out of his ears. He threw his hands up in the air and looked at my mum. She said she was looking after her sick kid and he said he'll be back.

Back then I didn't know why Dimos the Boss came to see my mum or what he wanted. But when I was trying to get her into treatment, I understood how Dimos and men like him had made her crazy.

⌗

I wondered if Mum might agree to go to the clinic if I could organise an appointment with a female doctor. I went to the clinic and spoke to another tired and sarcastic receptionist. When I asked to talk to a female doctor, the receptionist looked at me like a weirdo creep. I told the receptionist that I wasn't a creep that I was actually gay and I was trying to see someone for my mum. With your kind its always about your mother, said the receptionist. I went and sat down.

After almost an hour, a nurse called my name. He was tall and easy on the eyes. Following him down the hall, I looked at his long hair tied up in a bun. The skin on the back of his neck was overly tanned; it looked much older than his face.

We went into a room with two sofas facing each other, over-looking a courtyard that was full of rocks. The nurse gestured towards one of the couches, and sat down opposite me with a clipboard in his hands. His dark jeans had a shine on them that indicated the denim was a Japanese selvedge, and he wore limited-edition sneakers in green and beige suede. His aesthetic was not from the suburbs and he had an earnest face looking for the good in people. A privileged guy who was slumming it by working this side of the tracks.

I explained the situation to him using the language I had learned from all the phone calls I had made. He told me to bring Mum in next week at this time. I asked if he understood that she could only see a female doctor. He said that he got it. Sitting on the couch, I sighed. My head felt lighter and my shoulders relaxed.

⊞

I told Mum about the female doctor we were going to see. That it was for the health of her soul. She agreed to meet this female doctor. We walked the twenty minutes through the suburb and Mum complained. I told her there was no bus from our house to the clinic. This was true, but even if there had been I would have preferred to walk; I didn't want her to get spooked by bus drivers, and I hoped the walk would tire her out, making her more cooperative when we saw the doctor. As we crossed the oval, she asked if this was the way to my primary school and I said no. I tried to take her hand and she said I was too old to hold her hand.

We got to the clinic ten minutes before our appointment. We were lucky because the waiting room was empty. My mum went and sat on a plastic chair; she put her hands under her bum when she sat down. She looked around the room, and then got up to grab one of the pamphlets in Greek. I told the receptionist that my mum had an appointment with the female doctor, and she told me to wait. I sat down next to Mum and asked her what the pamphlet said. She looked up at me suspiciously and said that she had forgotten how to read.

We sat there for ten minutes, watching staff use their electronic swipes to get through the heavy clinic doors and disappear inside. No one turned to look at us. My mother started tapping each of her fingers on her elbows as she looked around. She stood up and took a few steps forwards and I asked her where she was going. Then the male nurse from the previous week walked past. He looked at me, and then at my mum pacing around the room. He swiped and went through the doors, and five minutes later a young doctor came out. She had a white coat and a heart-shaped face. My mum bowed to her and asked her if she was Vietnamese. I smiled because I was embarrassed. The doctor politely asked my mum to go with her. My mum wiped her hands on her clothes, nodded and followed the doctor through the clinic doors.

When Mum came out again she introduced me to the doctor, who was only a few years older than me. Under her white coat she wore a knee-length skirt and her shoes were pink ASICS. She cocked her head when we shook hands. Her face was calm and pleasant, and my mum looked happy. In Mum's hand was a plastic jar of pills, and I asked her what she had there. Some pills for my soul.

The doctor thanked me for bringing my mum in. She played with a wedding ring while we spoke. My shame grew, standing there being introduced by my mum to a psych doctor. Although I was taller than the doctor, I felt much smaller than her. We were the same age, but she could offer my mother something I couldn't.

Me and Mum left the clinic. I said, That went well, and she disagreed. On the way home I asked her if she liked the doctor. She said yes, she liked her very much, but the pills weren't going to fix her. We were walking along a residential street. A businessman in a car turning into a driveway waited and waved us across. As soon as we had passed he pulled into his carport.

At the oval, kids were doing soccer training in blue-and-white uniforms and their fathers watched from the sideline. The kids wore coloured socks pulled up to their knees and ran backwards around orange witches' hats. The fathers wore thick black parkers and huddled in packs. It was the local Greek soccer team called the Minotaurs. Their team mascot was a muscled bull. Mum's ears pricked up as we passed them. One of the soccer dads kept saying the word *putana*. Mum's eyes darted from side to side and her shoulders hunched. She dug into her pocket, pulled out the plastic jar and threw it away.

25.

Frenchie the French bulldog was barking and I was trying to watch a web series called *Married Without Children* at my desk. The series is set in a 1950s-style kitchen with a vintage dining set and cupboards painted aqua, and the main characters are called Jason and Medea. Medea wears a polka-dot swing skirt cinched at the waist and Jason has black pants, white shirt and a skinny tie. There's a vague story arc following their daily hijinks after the death of their children, as they try to deal with the appropriate etiquette of what to say to the coroner and avoid the question of who killed the kids.

The show got a bit heavy, especially when Medea had to order two child-sized coffins, so I went to the kitchen to make a coffee. Stuck to the middle of the fridge door was Mem's photo of the back of my head, with a note attached to it: Hot for a Muslim? Kane must have got a copy of the photograph from Lorna. His handwriting was all straight lines, ready for business. The attempt at humour in this message was neutralised by the seriousness of his hand writing.

I stood staring at the photo for a while. My hands were holding on to the chain-link fence and my arms were bent at a perfect ninety-degree angle, enhancing the slight musculature of my shoulders and back revealed by the singlet. My hair had just been cut. It was a striking photo – anyone looking at it would find this person attractive. I was glad that Kane had a copy of it and that he had put it up in pride of place.

Kane was out for the day and I could pretend I owned the house. Frenchie was in the backyard, and when I'd made my coffee I went outside to drink it with him. He had been lying under a small bush but ran up to me when I opened the sliding door. I put down my coffee, squatted and took his face in my hands. I rubbed his body all the way up and down. The thin black skin over his torso reminded me that he was leaner than me, leaner even than Kane. What a bitch! To have a lower BMI than me! Our faces were inches apart and I cooed at him. Frenchie's jowls dripped saliva and his bug eyes looked directly at me. He looked at me the same way Kane did – with expectation that I would make his life more convenient.

Bark! Get me food! Bark! Take me for a walk! Bark! Pretend to be an Albanian Muslim! Most of his body was black but his face was discoloured, with patches of grey under his button nose. Kane explained that this defect had made him cheaper than the rest of his litter. Frenchie was a bargain, a replica of a real French bulldog.

Frenchie ran away from me and spun around in a circle three times. He had an insect face and the personality of an excitable teen. I never understood gay men's fascination with French bulldogs until I had the pleasure of seeing firsthand their toy-like features, like their button faces and their human-bred disabilities.

When I'd finished my coffee, I put Frenchie in his rainbow harness and attached the rainbow leash to take him for a walk.

As we walked towards the lake I got a phone call from Lorna. She called out my name three times in a row and asked if I was asleep. Her voice ran down my ear and into my muscles. Every time she spoke, I felt like I was under orders and it made me want to yell. In a slow voice I told her that I was taking the dog for a walk.

Lorna told me that Cliff's article about me had been published online. It appeared on the *Pink Triangle Times* just under a listicle titled 'Six of the Hottest Bushrangers in Australian History'. She said not to worry because the bushrangers they listed weren't that hot – most of the pictures were unflattering old-timey police arrest photos. I said that in an era when the gay community was divided into the trinity of Yas Queens, Masc Jocks and Scruffos there will always be a market for Ye Olde Outlaw. I pointed out that if the bushrangers could have taken selfies there would be photos of them standing shirtless in a bathroom looking at their camera phone with their brow furrowed.

The headline above my own photo read 'Gay Muslim Fears for Life with New Mosque'. So far the article had been shared almost two hundred times, and gay men across Australia were posting comments about it. I asked Lorna to read them out to me. These people are savages, said one. The sword of Islam versus the rainbow flag, said another – that could have been Kane himself. This poor handsome man, someone wrote, despite the fact that my face wasn't shown. I'll give him a new home, said another. And the last comment was: I prefer uncut cock. The comments reminded me how quick netizens are to take on the role of moral authority. Yet even when the outrage is genuine, and not just virtue-signalling, empathy is only extended to those who share similar qualities. The gays were coming out as valiant defenders of the terrified Albanian, but only because they felt that a part of their own identity was being threatened.

Frenchie started barking, and I heard wheels scraping on concrete. I turned to see three horrible pre-teens approaching on Razor scooters, the sun reflecting off their chrome handles. Frenchie stood staunch, his barking becoming frenzied. All three boys had smooth pre-pimple faces but the cruel eyes of adolescents looking for fun. In my ear, Lorna asked what that sound was and if I was still there. I put the phone down at my side and picked up Frenchie with one hand. The three boys razored directly at me and I stood my ground. Just when they were about to crash into me, they swerved. I put the dog down and he jumped around my feet, barking. One of them said, Nice leash. I put the phone back up to my ear and told Lorna it was just boys being boys.

I kept walking, past the empty lot where Mehmet had taken the photographs. Lorna told me the article was being shared on people's Facebook pages, and according to the analytics over three thousand people had clicked on it. I asked what the impact on council would be. She said she had promoted it through her social media and the outrage comments had started.

When I got to the lake, I sat on a bench in front of the marshes. While Lorna told me what the next stage of the campaign would entail, a man walked past pushing a stroller. It looked like the same kind of stroller that Lorna owned. He had taken it off road and it was doing fine on the grass. I saw many pramfaces in the area, but they were mostly women. This man wore a white singlet made from technical fabric; his arm had a one-sitting Japanese sleeve tattoo. The colours were rich, the flowers done in red and the fish in gold. Running down his right leg below his Adidas shorts was a Pacific-style tattoo with geometric shapes and lines running diagonal.

Seeing him, Frenchie wagged his nub, his nose twitching. I wrapped my hand around the leash just as Frenchie pulled towards the man. The man looked over and our eyes met. I held his gaze for a second and smiled. I interrupted Lorna to ask if her husband had any tattoos and she said yes. I said that it seemed he just walked past me, and Lorna told me that his name was Jim, not James or Jimmy, and that he had a Poly tatt on his leg and an expensive Japanese sleeve. I asked if he had Japanese or Pacific heritage and she said no. I kept on looking at him as he walked away, eye-banging him.

Despite the tatts he was an attractive man. His shoulders swelled out of his singlet and the material hugged his narrow waist. The line of his arse appeared as a crease in his shorts. On one side of him was the manmade lake and on the other were the brand-new houses. He fitted perfectly into that environment, his random choice of cultural tatts as artificial as the landscape around him.

⊞

At lunchtime I leaned against the kitchen bench and munched on a chicken salad out of a stainless-steel bowl. As I ate I looked at the photo on the fridge. Seeing a photograph of yourself is getting a letter written in bullet points of your beauty and faults.

Looking at my hotness made my chest expand and I stopped leaning on the bench. I rocked back on my heels and stabbed the chicken salad confidently with my fork. No loser there! The four syllables were drumbeats in my head, Kane's language absorbed into my brain.

I pictured Kane standing with one hand on his hip and the other pointing to empty air. Losers! he would say, referring to the general public. They're all losers! I repeated the words. I had never had a male authority figure in my life, so whenever I met one I usually turned around and dropped my pants. But with Kane, I also listened to him. A male receptionist was either a fembot or a loser. Correct! A barista who put caramel syrup instead of hazelnut in his skim latte was a total loser. Bingo! Objects fell into this binary as well: if the coffee machine didn't perforate the Nespresso pod on the first try then it was a loser too. Stupid!

I was sipping mineral water out of a highball glass with ice and cucumber slices when Kane came home. He carried a pile of his shirts, just pressed at the drycleaners. Blue, white and pink wrapped in clear plastic. He dumped them on the table and hung his LV messenger bag over the back of a chair. He unbuttoned his aquamarine button-down Oxford shirt all the way to his waist. His chest was smooth and dotted with freckles; when he turned away my eyes ran over the sun lines on the back of his neck. Leather neck. He told me about his workday. When he'd microwaved his macro meal in the kitchen at lunchtime, the office gays were appraising the strengths and weaknesses of each *Real Housewives* franchise.

I tried to focus on his eyes but kept looking at the line in the middle of his chest that defined his pecs. Glowing nips fell out of his shirt. He held a green bottle and poured an arc of mineral water into a glass. Even though he was a freelancer, the office gays had already taken him under their wing. They discussed the poor gay Albanian Muslim they'd read about in the *Pink Triangle Times*, and suggested a consumer boycott of all the businesses associated with the local council. Kane encouraged them to share the article on social media. It's your way of doing something for the community, Kane apparently said to the loser fembots. I asked how the article was spreading online and Kane pulled it up on his phone to read some of the commentary on it.

This isn't the Middle East – welcome to Oz! was one comment by a social media loser who shared his hot takes like he shared his shirtless selfies. Other keyboard warriors had tagged council directly into their posts that said Not in Our Backyard! They had found random people who worked for council and bravely confronted them online. On John Smith's Facebook page, people who didn't even know him posted the article asking him to explain himself and council. Someone else posted a link to the article with eight question marks in a row. John Smith's title was Volunteer Liaison Officer and he had nothing to do with zoning, but that didn't stop the men who had applied causes filters to the profile photos on their social media pages.

As he was telling me this, Kane got a call from Lorna. He relayed the information to me as they talked. She told him that council had announced it would be discussing the mosque at its next meeting. The press release emphasised that the safety of all community members was extremely important to council, as was its relationship to responsible corporations. Community outrage had turned into the threat of consumer boycotts; dollars spoke when screams were muffled. Kane hung up the phone. He smiled, teeth clenched, the ends of his mouth reaching to his ears.

Kane pointed at the picture on the fridge. He went to the living room and took out a coffee-table book called *Urbanista Muertos*, which had photos of standard hot gays posing in landscapes in various states of decay. Lone nude bodies were plopped in empty factories and decomposing houses. There was a close-up of a dangling cock pressed against the exposed bricks of what was shown in the next photo to be a crumbling smoke stack. In another picture a man with cum gutters lay in a gutter; the text at the bottom of the page read, 'We are all in the gutter, but some of us are looking up at the cocks.' In the next picture it showed the exact same image, except for a thin yellow stream falling onto the man's face.

I was looking at the pictures when I felt my body stir. Kane's cock must have moved too. He flipped through a few more pages and put the book down. The air became still, and I was aware of his breathing. I put the tips of my fingers under the glossy page to turn it, and then he ambushed me.

His hand grabbed my flank to spin me around. I looked up at him and our eyes met. He bent his head down; I opened my mouth and his tongue landed on my upper palate. He pushed his hips into me, seized my wrists and held them in a vice-like grip. I counterattacked by darting my tongue in and out of his mouth. He unbuttoned my jeans, then turned me around again so my arse was pressed against his crotch. His right arm snaked around my chest and his left wrapped around my waist. He pushed the backs of my legs with his knees and marched me into his bedroom.

It was the first time I'd entered his bunker since I'd been living there. Inside was a black tallboy and a white cupboard; a mirror was placed strategically where the headboard was. On a white bedside table was a lamp with a black base and white shade. The doona was a crosshatch pattern and there was a dust ruffle around the bed. The dust ruffle reminded me that there is often an overlap between middle-aged gay men and grandmothers. Above the bed were three framed black-and-white photos of artsy disembodied male parts.

I looked straight ahead at the photos. Kane wrenched my jeans down to my knees and used his foot to press down on the crotch of the jeans while I stepped out of them. I kneeled on the bed and arched my back to push out my arse. He pressed his face into my rear, and my shock came out as a moan. His tongue wormed into me, poking in and out. I closed and opened my eyes, catching glimpses of the photos above his bed. A man's smooth glutes were captured in ultra close-up: slight fluff where the cheeks met the legs, the lower back muscles popping. My crotch rose, and I played with my dick. Kane spun me onto my back, pinned down my arms and licked my chest. He kissed my nipples and then sucked on them. I pushed his head away, worried I might get a rare case of male lactation. Above me, I focused on the pec photo, zoomed into the small dark nipple. I noticed the ring of fine hairs around it.

Kane moved to my underarm. No! Don't! I said, remembering that I hadn't put on deodorant, but he pushed his face deeper into my pit. I heard his muffled voice say, I love it, and I laughed and looked up. The last photo showed a man's underarm, the arm held out to the side. Suddenly I realised that those photos weren't just there to be admired; they were a map to Kane's sex life. Was this how he had sex with everyone? Bum, nips, pits and then free-form improvisation?

When he was on top of me, Kane thrust extra hard and his face turned into a red ball. After finishing in me, he fell off and nestled into the bed. I hadn't orgasmed, but he closed his eyes and rolled onto his side. His breathing became slower and deeper until his whole body vibrated with snores. I got out of bed and looked back at him lying there; his flesh was a series of mounds and angles. The tribal tattoo was a scribble on his body and his snores were a soundtrack to my exit.

I washed Kane's scent off my body and went for a walk. When my dick deflated, the energy swirled around my insides; it shuddered a column that ran up and down my body. My animus swirled on my skin, ran down my fingers and made my eyes jump. My brain leaped from thought to thought: Go for a walk in quicksand! Eat something you find in the street! Do push-ups in the middle of the footpath!

A hot wind blew between the houses. Sweat collected between my thighs and I plucked at the material of my shorts, pulling it away from my skin. I walked through the suburb until the sun was landing on the edge of roofs.

I found myself outside a house I had never noticed before, though I must have passed it many times. A Jeep was parked out front, its left wheels up on the kerb. The facade of the single-storey house was divided in two: one side had a high-pitched gable roof with double bay windows underneath and a doorway behind a superfluous charcoal-black arch; the other side had a slanted roof above a two-car garage.

The garage door was rolled up halfway; fluorescents glowed inside. It was the movement of a figure under the light that caught my eye. Facing a boxing bag, he punched out four jabs in a row and then delivered a sharp shin-kick to the bag. As he repeated the sequence, it made a drumbeat. *Thud, thud,*

thud, *thud*, and *smack*. I noticed the familiar markings on his body, the colour-block inks of a Japanese sleeve and the angled geometry of a Poly-style tattoo on his leg.

I squatted just behind the front fence and rested my elbows on my legs to watch him. He had a classic ectomorph body type that had been refined with lots of high-impact cardio. His legs were two little sticks below knee-length basketball shorts. Every crinkle of his musculature was visible, and his spine pushed up through his skin. At the end of each sequence he spun around to do a set of burpees, and his mouth was a tiny slit which his tongue would fall out of as he panted. His lateral muscles were close to his body and they looked like gills.

He was so focused on his workout that he didn't notice me crouching there. I took a waddle towards him. He continued his routine. Punches on the bag, a shin-hit and a set of burpees. Sweat pooled under his arms as he moved through each sequence. The shine on his face turned into micro rivers, drops spattering the concrete around him. My legs shuddered in the squat, my torso wobbled, and my palms hit the ground before my body did, slapping on the driveway, intertwining with the sounds coming from the garage.

I looked up but he was still unaware of me. As he began another circuit I took a few steps back; the fluorescent light escaped from the garage and fell across the driveway in a rectangle. The *thud*, *thud*, *thud*, *thud* and *smack* against the bag, his body falling down into a rock-hard plank, squeezing his body into the shape of a ball and then back out, stiffly, into the plank. Then the quick rhythm of up and down, up and down – *hit, hit, hit* – and the release of liquid falling all over the concrete.

26.

Basil kept wanting to meet at the cafe next to Vas Bros Real Estate. At first I thought he was committed to their macchiatos, but after meeting him there a few times I realised that the cafe was a set where he could play a starring role.

Basil stood in the spotlight, next to the coffee machine talking to Barista Girl. She wore Clubmaster glasses, her messy brown ponytail peasant-girl long. Her black T-shirt was a size too big and was speckled with coffee grounds. Basil held a toffee-coloured Royal Republiq soft leather briefcase in front of him. He was wearing a snug blazer and pants combo in blue with a silver sheen; he was a disco ball among all the matte sweats. A midday yoga mum sitting at a nearby table raised her head from reading her phone and drank Basil in.

She stared so long that she almost forgot why she'd looked up in the first place. Her head tilted. Aware that she had been looking too long, she turned her attention back to her phone and then waved down another skinny latte.

I walked up and tapped Basil's shoulder. He spun around and said, Look what we got here, eh! He performed for the young woman, his voice singsong. He grabbed my shoulder and turned to introduce me to her. This guy right here, he said, dragging me forwards, this guy is writing a book about me. He's a writer. Basil's eyes shone at Barista Girl. She put a metal jug under the steam nozzle and it farted through the milk. Smiling politely with her mouth closed, she told Basil that it sounded nice. The three of us stood there, the two men standing at the counter and the woman working away, chained to the machine, trying to get on with her job.

Keeping up his shark grin, Basil patted me on the shoulder, three taps, each tap ending with a squeeze. As he squeezed he made a follow-up statement. You know what? He's a faggot. Been friends since high school.

My mouth dropped open, and Barista Girl looked over at me. Basil was showing off; the subtext was that he was progressive and cool with the gays. She grimaced, and I shrugged. Basil's hand dropped off my shoulder, and when he spoke again his tone had changed. Just bring us two macchiatos, he said. She sighed, and I saw that she had been through this kind of interaction a thousand times before, and was fed up with men peacocking for her attention.

We walked towards the back of the cafe and Basil kept his briefcase in front of him. I complimented him on it and he said that it was handy to hide his erection when he spoke to young women.

As we sat down Basil took out his laptop and said that he was going to look over his calendar as we spoke. Imma multitasker! Barista Girl arrived with the coffees in half-sized translucent glasses on brown saucers and asked if we could make room on the table. I took my elbows off the tabletop and Basil pushed his laptop to the side, revealing the screen to me.

As the young woman put Basil's coffee in front of him, he grabbed her arm just above the wrist. There were brown hairs growing back over his knuckles, the laser hair removal must have not been strong enough. The orange colour of his hand pressed against the milk white of her skin. She took a sharp breath in and looked at Basil. He said, Sugar would be necessary, please. The soft tones of his voice, the syrupy way he said 'sugar' and the odd word 'necessary' made the girl look at Basil, crinkles on her forehead. He let go of her hand and she walked away, shook her arm and reached towards her hair to smooth it down.

I pulled out my phone to record our conversation. Barista Girl came back and dropped the packets of sugar on the table. Her face had changed from polite girl-in-the-service industry to stone. As she walked off, Basil said he needed to take a slash and got up. He left his computer on, the screen still facing me. He'd opened up the calendar with his colour-coded schedule. A piece of information stood out. Another appointment at Keating's Storage World.

When I saw the name on Kamilla's laptop it sparked at me and I took a photo of it. My understanding of Basil's job was that he lived in offices and meetings, he organised deals, he got finance and managed people. Since when do property developers need to pick up equipment? I turned the laptop around so it was no longer facing me.

Basil returned to the table and sat down. He picked up the sugar satchels and delicately ripped them; brown crystals fell onto the milk foam of the macchiato. With two fingers he lifted the coffee cup, slurp-sipped it and gently whirled it around.

Just then Barista Girl emerged from the toilet. Her hands hung at her sides and her eyes were dead. I hadn't seen her go to the bathroom, and I suddenly realised that Basil must have followed her in. As she walked past, I made a deliberate show of looking at her, making sure that Basil knew that I clocked something went down. She darted past our table and turned her face away. What did you do to her? I asked Basil.

Nothing, said Basil. I just got her number, bro. Told her I wanted to be friends.

27.

Instead of writing I opened the top drawer of my writing desk and pulled out a pamphlet. This pamphlet is sent out with all Australian passports. Everyone gets one, people going to see the *Mona Lisa* in the Louvre and people taking sex tours of South-East Asia.

In green text on the front of the pamphlet are the words SMART HINTS FOR AUSTRALIAN TRAVELLERS. Underneath the words is a picture of a man lying on a deckchair, with a bright sky and palm trees mid-sway. The fresh green and white of the brochure sparked holiday desires. With my index finger I traced the man's arm holding the tropical drink to the sky. I rubbed my thumb where his leg crossed over his other knee. I wanted to be in the picture: relaxed because I was lying down, relaxed because I was half drunk in the sun, and safe because I was a Smart Traveller and before I flew I had looked in the top drawer of my writing desk and pulled out a pamphlet to inform myself about the dangers outside of Australia.

On page thirty-one opposite a picture of hands with different skin tones piling on top of each other is information on laws relating to and attitudes towards LGBTQI travellers around the world. According to the brochure, homosexuality is not illegal in Albania but is frowned upon. You could say this of Australia or Greece, the two countries that I belong to. You could also say that being a homosexual is not illegal in Pemulwuy, nor is it frowned upon, but if you walked around like a faggot, holding another faggot's hand being a big faggy mess you probably would get bashed, especially if your glitter shorts matched your harness. Every time I looked at the Smart Traveller guide I wanted to go somewhere I could walk around and be gay in public. Images scrolled through my brain: compartmentalised aeroplane food, Bintangs on the beach, Mykonos in speedos, jacuzzis in the shape of Buddha, resort wear patterned with exotic flowers, fern-side massages, and the sea of red roofs that people see when they fly out of Sydney.

I placed the guide back in the drawer. Giving up on my aeroplane dreams, but still wanting to avoid writing, I decided to take a walk around Pemulwuy. Carpet in the hallway outside my room cushioned my soles; my heavy footprint left an indent. With each step, the synthetic polymers scratched at my feet.

It was the synthetic carpet, it was the replica Noguchi coffee table, it was the couches from Matt Blatt. It was the widescreen TV. It was serving platters and designer jugs. It was Frenchie the French bulldog and northern sun hitting the sliding doors. All of it was a home. One of the first homes I'd had in a long time. And even if I couldn't take off in a plane, I had somewhere to come back to after a walk.

Kane hovered between the kitchen and the living room, yelling with a Bluetooth in his ear. He complained that even though the money was good, he hadn't had time to get his PrEP script refilled and he was worried he might have got AIDS from having sex on a public toilet seat. I bent down to put on my shoes, flinching each time Kane said fuck; he hit that word so hard. I sat on the table, bum on the hard surface, from the bowl I picked up a piece of fake fruit and rolled it around my palm. I was waiting to ask if he wanted to come for a walk, where we could cruise for strangers by the lake.

Kane speaking on his Bluetooth, always hammed up the Aussie drawl. He elongated the word 'mate' with three *a*'s. There was enough space in the syllable to park a ute in there. Australians have so many different kinds of accents that it made it hard to contextualise people. I had to learn that the broad Australian accent, the one that people around the world associate with Crocodile Dundee, didn't necessarily mean the person owned a leather vest. Once, I was having drinks with a potential date in a suit bar in the city on a Friday night. When I closed my eyes I heard the voices of blue-collar workers; when I opened them I saw men in Zegna suits, tumblers of scotch in their hands. Hearing Kane's accent, and seeing him in his mesh gym singlets with his tattoo visible, and his oval wrap-around Oakley sunglasses, I would have guessed he was a security guard (false) on his day off, one who distributed meth (sometimes true).

When the conversation was over, he hit the Bluetooth on his ear. I was just about to speak when he held up one finger at me. There was something I needed to know. The campaign against the mosque was reaching the next level: gays had started targeting the advertisers who sponsored the council's Australia Day festival, and the companies were threatening to pull out. There would be no mosque now.

I held up a ceramic apple in victory. Kane kept speaking. He said that he was going to sell the house now, it had been the primary reason that he needed to stop the mosque in the first place. He told me I needed to pack up all my stuff and look for another place to rent; he was going to buy a single bedder closer to the city.

The apple fell out of my hand, dropped a few centimetres onto the table. Kane picked it up and put it back into the bowl. It was a busy day for him, gym and doctor. He told me he needed to get a PrEP refill even though doctors are now just antidepressant pez-dispensers. There was a rolled towel and a bottle of water under his arm. As he walked away, he reached around and scratched his back, lifting his shirt to expose the top of his Calvin Klein underwear.

It felt like a flash grenade had gone off; I sat still in the kitchen. Now that there was no mosque and the property prices would stay high, I could see that my changeling identity had been used for Kane's benefit. I had thought we were fighting together, not so that Kane could sell up and climb the property ladder.

I thought I belonged in that Pemulwuy house with Kane. Counting our macros with Middle Eastern-themed meals. A French bulldog scratching at the door. Comfort to me was a little box of drug paraphernalia and the scent of Nespresso coffees in Bodum double-wall glasses. No more watching his body do Hindu push-ups; from now on everything would be moving boxes.

My body came out of its frozen state. I ran towards the door. Kane! I have something to tell you!

He stopped at the front entrance and turned around. I ran up to him, hugged him and whispered something in his ear in a language he didn't understand. I put my forehead on his forehead, held it there for a while, and then turned around and walked away.

Back in my room I opened the desk drawer again. Next to the pamphlet of Smart Hints for Australian Travellers was a blue evil eye. I picked it up, held the glass ball in my fingers and balanced it back and forth.

28.

During university I moved out of the apartment me and my mother lived in. But after a month or two of living with flatmates, I would inevitably get a call from Mum's greasy landlord. Rent no pay for two weeks! What doing 'bout this? What, huh, is doing? His voice was half untrustworthy, half booming aggression and all typical sleaze-estate guy.

At uni one day I received one of these calls from the landlord and went straight to my mother's place.

The bus took me directly there and I briskly walked to the apartment block. As I walked up the final flight of stairs I saw the door slightly ajar. A sneaky eye peered at me through the frame and then the door swung open to reveal my mother.

She was wearing a red, faded singlet dress with an unstitched, fraying hemline. She stood erect, holding either side of the doorframe. Her legs were shoulder-width apart and a gust of air came from behind and blew against her dress, creating an outline of her body. Long strands of grey hair covered her face and blew in the draft. She extended her arm out and pointed at the apartment door opposite. Oh! she said, I dread to think of what is hatching in their mind.

I used to get embarrassed when she said horrible things about our neighbours, especially when they could hear. But the embarrassment disappeared, and I was just sad that she felt a need to hurt others verbally.

I walked past her into the apartment and riffled through old piles of newspapers and envelopes on top of a broken television until I found the details of her bank account. When I found the jumble of numbers, I realised that I needed to make changes in her life. After the failed attempt at improving her mental health, I could at least make her living arrangements easier.

On a day that I wasn't at uni, I spent too long with my ear to the receiver, easy listening music playing as I waited to speak to someone in Department of Housing about my mother's needs as a client. It was pure tedium waiting for government services, so I tried to slow my heartbeat to a *da-num da-num da-num* to save energy. The sad sounds of Dolly Parton's 'Jolene' were interrupted by a recorded announcement in a fatherly man's voice about the latest ways the Department of

Human Services was streamlining. I understood that stream-lining meant a reduction of services and I wanted to plead with the government, Please don't take them just because you can. The Department of Human Services treated the people of this state like something they had to manage, like rivers or oceans. Never say the polis is dead, merely that the people are a giant lug of biological obstacles who need to be served, watered, grown or dammed.

Eventually I got through to someone and asked about any available vacancies for public housing. She told me that they needed to speak directly to my mother. I said that her English wasn't good enough, and the woman paused for a second and asked how long she had been in the country. I said she had been in the country for thirty something years and the woman on the other end of the phone asked me again why she couldn't speak English. It wasn't really a question, so I hung up.

Then the solution came to me. I would call back a few days later pretending to be my mother. But first I had to practise. The character I developed, Me Mum, was a composite of all the stereotypes of Greek women. Me Mum rolled her *r*'s. Me Mum shortened vowels and elongated consonants.

Hitting the right pitch was hard because when I first started to practise, my voice went too high. I sounded like a husband impersonating his wife nagging him, one of the rituals of heterosexuality. Instead I focused on making my voice breathier, slowing down my speech and creating more space between each word.

When doing an impersonation of someone else, it's also important to use appropriate content. In the midst of conversations with representatives from the Department of Housing I would start talking about how my child didn't eat enough and this added to my worries: He no like taramasalata! I used the word 'worried' a lot, because Greek women are always worried. I would come up with a folksy metaphor comparing my own personal housing crisis to the difficulties of making tzatziki. One time when the representative asked why I was so out of breath and kept pausing between words, I said I had just finished doing an hour of Greek dancing.

There was an enjoyment in pretending to be someone else. I was trying to get my mum into government housing and get someone else to pay her bills. It was not lost on me that I was attempting to prove her diminished responsibility by becoming a Greek cliché.

I mastered Me Mum to scam the government and then I had to collect all her documents. In my real life, I told everyone about my predilections for minimalism because growing up with a mother who had hoarding tendencies made me think that placing sentimental meaning on objects was a weakness. Maybe I took this too far, throwing out too much. Thinking that the tattered teddy bears of my childhood were an Achilles heel. And maybe I took a completely modernist ideology that was only meant for aesthetics and applied it to the morality of humanity, the way the German state did before World War II or the way Australia does with its offshore processing. But after I made the decision to get Mum into public housing, I began to keep relevant documents with the precision of an archivist.

After I debuted Me Mum I found myself squatting among the piles of newspapers and plastic bags, where there were letters from government departments that certified Mum's income. Each time I found an important letter, I would categorise it appropriately. In a black plastic folder, I put letters from doctors, prescription notes and a copy of her case file from her one-off visit to the mental health clinic at the hospital. I sent them to the relevant people.

It took a while to make phone calls, organise forms and write letters. Eventually, she got offered a residence in Carramar by the river. It was a one-bedroom house in a block that had that 1960s public housing feel. Just beyond the houses was a walking track surrounded by long grasses and tall gums, it seemed too nice to be in Western Sydney – or at least undeserving of the people in public housing.

Online, I organised her bills to be automatically withdrawn from her bank account. The men in her head kept chasing her, but I had finally retired Me Mum and could start the hunt for cardboard moving boxes.

29.

I walked through the suburb and told myself that I was looking for cardboard boxes or storage containers, so I could pack my stuff for moving out of Kane's house. Night birds had started their songs, and a wind pushed their melodies over the letterboxes.

One of the houses had big open windows and a superfluous arch over the front entrance; it cast a shadow on the ground and I thought I saw a box or a laundry basket against the wall. The blinds were closed but TV light flickered around the edges. I took a few steps into the yard. When I got closer to the house, I saw that the object I'd noticed was a cube-shaped pot that was yet to be filled with a plant. I crouched down next to it and ran my finger over the ceramic glaze. I imagined the family who lived here excitedly deciding to fill it with a Wollemi pine.

In 1994 an adventurous bushwalker with a knowledge of plants wandered into a sandstone gorge in the Blue Mountains to the west of Sydney. He found a cluster of trees that had the fronds of a fern but the trunks of pines, large and ancient, and he took a clipping from one. He sent it to the right experts, who pronounced that it was the sole surviving species of its genus and its closest relative had become extinct almost two million years ago. The trees in that gorge were then protected and declared living fossils. In a bid to promote it, a propagation strategy was created to ensure the Wollemi pine was represented in botanic gardens around the world and as a potted substitute for Christmas trees in Australia. Throughout the Australian suburbs, this ancient species, rare and delicate, now grows among the Hills hoists, lawnmowers and buffalo grass.

The light around the rim of the blinds created a frame which drew me towards it. At the window I leaned against the wall. From this vantage point I could see a slither of the interior. There was a corner of grey modular and the back of a woman's head with a high ponytail. The television was screening a cooking show. A man walked into the room. In his arms were two brown pizza boxes. He must have just got home before I noticed the house. I couldn't see his head, but he wore a collared activewear polo and shorts, his stomach a slight hump under his shirt. His arms extended outwards, offering the pizza boxes to ponytail in a gesture that verged on a holy ritual. Her two white arms took the boxes and the man spun around and sat down next to her. He moved quickly, so I missed his face, but I saw the back of his head, hair grown out around the neck, meeting with black hair sprouting from his back.

Pizza boxes on laps, both heads leaned forwards and disappeared from my vision. The heads reappeared in their prime TV-watching spots and hands held pizza slices and moved them to mouths. The man ate a meat lovers slice and the woman ate a vegetarian one. I rested my head on the brick and felt the grit of sand on my cheek. I brushed it off.

A teenage boy walked in towards the two figures, sat down in front of them and disappeared. I moved to the other side of the window to get a better view of him and the rest of the family unit. My forehead almost touched the glass, my single eye looking straight into the living room. I saw them all, the mother and father sitting on the modular sofa, the teenager at their feet. Behind them was a black Kallax shelving unit from Ikea. One of the shelves was filled with cookbooks and the rest held a stereo system and commemorative plates. The family ate slowly, passing each other slices, and laughed in unison at the television. The father ruffled the boy's hair as he ate, and the boy's head swayed so much he coughed while eating the pizza. My eyes were drawn to the boy, a too-skinny teen with a over-washed shirt hanging off his body.

All of that, that family, made me turn around to face the street. I leaned back against the brick wall. I looked across the street, and the letterboxes, the awnings, the fences all blurred and disappeared underwater. I started crying, closed my eyes and put my face in my hands and the blackness swirled into sparkles. I saw a family of three heads: mother, father, son. I saw that skinny teen in wire-rimmed glasses. Smiling and eating, content to be at home. Happy with his limited family in a way that I wasn't when I was a teenager. And then I saw me as a teenager peering into people's homes, hoping that just by looking, the secret to their happiness would be imparted to me. And I wondered what was in me that was so wrong, that needed to look into people's homes to understand them.

Night silence was broken by the distant roll of skateboards and Razor scooters. I leaned over and spat in the empty glazed pot, putting my DNA in the base. I straightened up, went down the driveway and began to walk along the street again before the wheelie gang could roll by and make me out in the shadows. As I walked towards the middle of the suburb I thought about that family trinity planting a Wollemi pine in the pot. I thought about the roots absorbing my DNA and that when it got bigger the family would decorate it with outdoor Christmas baubles every December and, somehow, I would be a part of them.

⊞

I had some nerves in the dark and sat on a bench, my fingers slipping in between the slats. The lake in front of me was paper-calm. I pushed the lower arch in my spine back and forth. Back and forth. Never comfortable. Night over the park, night over the streets of Pemulwuy. As I heard my own breath, tiny wheels scraped against concrete. I inhaled the night air and the wind breathed out over me, over the bench, over the grasses. Rolling wheel sounds – *zzz zzz* – carried across the neighbourhood. The sounds bounced off stucco walls, the rolling wheels – *zzz zzz* – became louder. I turned my head to look for Razor scooters.

Up the street I saw them: stainless-steel stem handlebars. There was a flock of these metal poles shining in the dark and they got closer. I could just make out the white soles of Janoski Nikes, stepping against asphalt and pushing off. Stems and soles. They came towards me, they turned a corner to go off down another street.

Reeds in the lake shook.

Behind me someone asked me the time.

Aye, mate, you know the time?

I turned around and there was a teen standing there, his shaved head made him look like a lightbulb made of flesh. His shirt was oversized, his shorts stopped above the knee.

Aren't you too young to be out currently?

⊞

Zzz zzz – flock Razor scooters return. Coming around corner. Coming towards me. I stand up. Group of teens rush towards me. Bone lightbulb head asking me the time. Step back, lose my footing, arse on the ground. A semicircle of teens around me. Who you been looking at? Why you been looking at people in the dark? Faggot! Creep! Weirdo! Step up to me. Ball fists. Cover my head with my arms. Cover my ears. What's it like being watched faggot!

Fist connects with left side of my head, keel to the side, shoulder hits ground. Roll onto face. Pull knees under torso. Turn into a ball. Foot kicks my side. Oh, you wanna see us naked? Fingernails tear shirt, fingernails tear shorts, fingernails rip clothes to ribbons. Everything goes small. I'm in a part of my mind they can't get to. Hope they don't clobber me with scooters or props. Arms rain on me. Legs kick my flank. Gee, I'm glad that they have the soft bodies of adolescents. Somehow naked. Wrapped in a ball. Knees bent up under my stomach. Cheek flat on concrete. Direct blows onto my arms. Shoe wounds my side. One of them puts his foot on my back. Pushes me down. Closer to the ground, compressed. I hear camera phones taking photos of me as someone stands on my back because he wants a trophy shot. Give us a thumbs-up! Breathing heap, filling with air.

Hitting stops. They walk off. Hear wheels roll away. I still wait there with my hands at my side, stomach folded over my knees, forehead touching the concrete.

⌗

Clothes tattered and pains in my thigh, chest, back, I limped down the middle of the street. The blood from my nose had dried up but I kept wiping it with the back of my hand. A red line ran from my wrist to the fingernail of my index finger. Water without feeling leaked from my eyes; I felt the drops run down my cheek and settle at my jawbone. It wasn't tears though. I knew that on some kid's phone existed an image of me naked. You couldn't see my face, I was just a ball of flesh that another kid had a foot on, his thumb held up to the camera.

Arriving back at the house, I saw a 'for sale' sign in our front yard and spat out blood. I rolled my head down and covered my face with my hands. It was a slow shuffle up the path, through the door. I walked straight into the shower. The water ran down on me and it was too hot, my nose started bleeding again. I leaned over and put my cheek flush against the tiles and I kept thinking about getting hit in the small of my back. I reached around to massage it. After rubbing it for a while the feeling came back. My hand spun the taps and I walked from the shower to my room, leaving a wet trail on the carpet. I detoured into Kane's room to get one of his extra-soft, extra-luxurious towels. A towel hung on the bedpost. I took it and dried the bottom half of my body. As I moved it up to my head, I realised that the towel smelled of cum. I wasn't drying my body with one of his fancy towels but with one that was reserved for his emissions.

30.

I had only two days to pack up my stuff and find a new place to live. My other goal was to recover, and not aggravate the bruises and cuts on my body. It hurt to bend over and lift things, but I didn't have much stuff. I looked online at small studio apartments, most of them boxy hovels. On a desperate morning I called Basil and told him I was looking for a place. He called me back half an hour later and told me he had found me a cheap but okay studio. I decided to take it without seeing it. The flat was on the outskirts of Bankstown, walking distance to the shops. I bandaged and covered all my cuts so they wouldn't split open when I moved

My life had become a primal hunt for cardboard boxes. I went to the alley behind the supermarket in Pemulwuy

Marketplace and checked the dock. People driving past saw a wog with a bruised eye, scratches all over his face, fat lips, and purple pools up his arm. I hovered around depots where trucks pulled up. A car slowed down to look at me and sped up when I glared at the driver. A staff member emerged from a back door and said, Can I help you, but it wasn't a question.

The day I moved into my studio apartment I needed Kane to help me carry the mattress up the stairs. It was hard to ask for his help. My top lip involuntarily curled every time he told me he was packed and ready to go, and I held back barbs when he said that he had hired movers for his own stuff. Flight by flight we breathed deeply and pushed and pulled the mattress up with our muscles. Kane was at the bottom of the mattress while I guided it from the top. Cobwebs on the windows caught my eye; I saw Kane look at them too. We took a breather halfway up the stairs. A hammock of cobwebs covered the corner of one window. My chest heaved and I looked at the flies and beetles caught in the web.

I angled the mattress and Kane pushed it through my door. I pointed to where I wanted it and we tipped it over. It landed on the floor and dust balls went flying across the room. Kane walked around the apartment looking at the fixtures. I asked if he would miss me and he changed the subject. He was going to inner Sydney, into one of those blocks of one-bedders with contemporary chrome appliances. Miele – finally! Smeg – no more loser whitegoods! The rubber soles of our sneakers ripped from the parquetry floor as we walked to the balcony.

I smoked a cigarette and Kane chastised me as we looked over the brown fence. My city view consisted of a main road and walls of bricks and balconies on the other side. Kids played in the grounds of the flats and screamed without joy. They rode tiny plastic bikes on concrete forecourts and played bullrush between four-storey buildings. I complained to Kane about having to fall asleep to the sounds of beeping rubbish trucks and the honking of cars backed up on the highway. Opposite us women stood on their balconies; they wore lounging hijabs and smoked argileh. Below them their toddlers rode plastic trikes in circles. Kane took off his shirt to get some rays. He stood so close to me that I thought we might get jihaded for being poofs. I noticed the freckles on his shoulder, where the sun had done its damage. I told him that I went to high school down the road. Well, fuck, you haven't gone far in life, he said. Kane told me that he was moving to inner Sydney. I said that it sounded grand, his chest rose and expanded with pride. The sun beat down on his white chest. He looked at the main road with its potholes, the shit-brick and concrete boxes of the flats, the children yelling and screaming below us and said that he was glad he wasn't coming back here.

⊞

The studio apartment was a glorified box with a wall dividing the main area in two. The main area included a big empty space where I put my mattress and desk. On the other side of the wall was a kitchen with a small bar fridge and a stovetop that plugged into an electrical outlet. I was happy to live there temporarily but it wasn't a place I could bring fancy boys.

The building contained a range of apartments: three bedroom, two bedroom and studio. I met the other tenants on the stairs. The old Greek man across the hallway worked in a chicken shop. At nights I would hear his shower running and his voice singing chants from the Byzantine Orthodox church while he scrubbed the smell of fried chicken off his body, and I was transported to the few times I had been to church with my mother. He had a wife who lived in Greece, who I never saw. He called her Soula and I told him I liked that name. It was the comforting way it rolled out of my mouth, the *o* rounding my tongue. It reminded me of my mum's friends and helped to heal the bruises that I still carried.

On the floor below my studio were two-bedroom apartments with families of six and seven people. They decorated their balconies with green and white bunting during Ramadan, left piles of shoes outside their doors and lit incense in the hallway. This upset the older white lady who lived by herself in the three-bedroom place on that floor. Sometimes I saw herds of children in the stairwell wearing blue and white; later I realised these occasions correlated to when the Bulldogs played well. Sounds wafted through the apartment building along with the smells of food. When I was home, I heard crying – it might have been a child or a woman. The closest I got to communicating with these families was brief waves as they left for their night-shift jobs in the afternoon.

When I walked to the shops I saw high school acquaintances. They still had a youthful cheer, but they were bald, fat, and had little shitlets running around them.

There was a pulse that started from my tailbone, shot up my spine and the back of my neck, hit the base of my skull, then spread through my brain and made my shoulders shudder. It started after the teens bashed me; my brain interpreted someone looking at me with a cocked head or squinting suspicion as punches to the back of my head or kicks to my side.

When I walked around the area, I was aware of the way people watched me, I felt their eyes on me. How did I present to the hi-vis Habibs who drove past in flatbed hunting trucks, looking out their windows at me? To the women walking with shopping bags? I wondered what they made of a man strolling along the footpath in activewear and sunglasses.

My skin was slowly starting to heal, cuts scabbing over. The bruises were still visible on my face, and my left arm was discoloured where I had tried to protect my head from the blows.

Before leaving the apartment I chose my outfit carefully, changing several times. I began with a collared polo shirt and tech shorts, then swapped the polo for a scoop-neck shirt. But the scoop neck was too low; it revealed the top of my chest and the hair on it. I settled on a blue crew-neck T-shirt. It strangled my neck, but it wouldn't attract attention.

I took my wallet and went down the stairs. On the bottom floor I bumped into my old Greek neighbour. He smelled of frying oil and he asked me if I was off to see my girlfriend. I laughed and replied, No. He stood there and repeated a bunch of clichés: Work is Work! and, Another Day, Another Dollar! I told him that I did all my work from home and he pointed up to the studio and asked if there was enough room up there. His voice was so deep in normal speech; it came from his feet and resonated through his overweight body. He patted down his shirt and said that he needed to have a shower. As he walked past, the odour rolled onto me; the only thing left of our interaction was his scent in my nostrils.

I turned around to watch him climb the stairs, leaning forwards, each footstep connecting with the floor. I wanted to go back upstairs to hear him singing; he would even sing Greek blues in a mashup of shower sadness.

I walked out past the letterboxes and looked up and down the street. The area was all apartment blocks, each four-storeys high. On the little patches of grass in front of them were discarded ancient fridges, mattresses and old sheets of asbestos. Anything and everything could be found in these piles. At one point I wondered if the Sydney Biennale had moved to

Bankstown – surely an artist had constructed these displays to critique consumerism using the post-apocalyptic debris abandoned on nature strips.

Today the sky was a sheet of grey clouds that muted the red bricks. A hot wind blew and people sat on balconies waiting for the clouds to break. I smelled the fruity aroma coming from the cheap deodorant I had used on my underarms.

One foot in front of the other. I worried about the way my arms moved. I held them slightly out from my body, to give the appearance of big shoulders and lateral muscles. I tugged on the neckline of my T-shirt. Wiping the nervous sweat from my forehead, I felt a bruise. I had decided that if anyone asked I would tell them it was a sex-related injury. Oh, this? This happened when I had to fight off people clawing at my peen!

Being invisible was a trick I had to re-master, and the way I was trying to master it was through imitation. I had to become what was expected on the street. I made a spreadsheet in my mind of all the men I saw. Thick-legged workers in hi-vis, real estate salesmen in polyester suits getting into Audis, and older men with beards and tracksuits. I took parts from each of them and put them on my body.

A bearded man in an orange vest was walking from his van to an apartment building. His legs were golden and hairless, in contrast to his full beard. The only way a man could have hairless blemish-free legs and a thick beard was if he had access to a master waxer or a cousin who worked in laser hair removal. I looked down at the line in his calf muscle and saw how his knees and toes pointed outwards – he walked heel first, his toes leading the way. I practised this for fifteen steps, but my knees started to ache from being turned out. Perhaps I was destined to have my awkward, femme gait for eternity, rendering me a victim of laughing teens and smacks across the head.

On reflection, too, that angled-arm lat walk wouldn't make me invisible. A lot of men in Bankstown walked this way, but they did it to take up room and draw attention to themselves. I needed to find gestures and mannerisms that made me fit in with the people around me, but without suggesting a macho aggressiveness.

As I walked towards the shops, the rows of apartment blocks gave way to houses. Bungalows on quarter-acre blocks, and duplexes with luxury cars parked in the driveways. Other houses had been changed from fibro shacks into brick-veneer-with-bay-windows; they had white concrete lions at the gates and statues of Mother Mary in the front garden. Growing up in wog areas, I knew that concrete front yards meant that the houses were inhabited by the post-World War II southern European migrants, ones that came to build Australia and who had decided that there could be no reminder of their agrarian past. Concrete replaced grass, white lions, balustrade and columns were a nod to the images of the ancestral lands and inside me, they became a part of my own personal architecture.

My imagination replaced my spine with a pillar. Immediately my back straightened, and the crown of my head lifted to the sky. I noticed all the women walking along the street. Elderly Muslim women pushing jingling Woolworths trolleys full of plastic bags. Older white women dragging tartan carriers with two wheels. A mother shepherding three kids, each of them lugging two plastic bags.

Usually, men appeared in the street only as they moved between the car and front door. There was the odd junkie walking shirtless in shorts. A young man in Under Armour with a backpack on his way to the gym. The men were always alone, in quick transit, and never carried shopping bags.

31.

In the middle of south-western Sydney is Bankstown. On one side of Bankstown the topography resembles a wide, low serving bowl – this area is imaginatively named Punchbowl. On the other side of Bankstown is a hill. A water tower now stands there, but before the water tower was built it was a place where bushrangers were hanged. This hill and bowl on either side of the suburb mean that water runs right through Bankstown. Clouds form above the hill, precipitation hits it, and the water streams through the suburb to settle in the bowl.

The people of Bankstown share the same transient, passing-through quality. No one here really looks 'Australiana'. Beer isn't popular. Blondes are mostly peroxide. Barbecues have gas bottles rather than charcoal and are found on the small balconies of apartments – even though it's illegal.

The population of Bankstown make it completely Western Sydney. Or rather I should say that it's the population's beliefs that make it completely Western Sydney. Here you can find people who believe in the magic ghosts of religion. Whether these be prophet or saviour. Pantheism is represented by the Hindu population. Even Buddhist animism fits in well, especially in this era when car navigation systems can communicate with drivers.

All things should be celebrated here. In Bankstown the men remove hair from their bodies as much as the women do. Everyone talks about the origins of the Illuminati as much as they talk about the origins of superheroes like Arnold Schwarzenegger from Hollywood.

Even though the population and their beliefs make it fit perfectly into Western Sydney, it's debatable if Bankstown is in Western Sydney. State government and councils have spent years fighting over which part belongs where. Much like the debates over whether Italians, Orthodox Greeks and Lebanese Maronites are still considered ethnic or whether they have become Anglo-adjacent. I thought the Italians had come closest to whiteness; they are adequately represented in government and media. But the other day I picked up a newspaper and read an article about a big family of Italians targeting Aussies on an Australian cruise liner. The family structure was described as a gang and the media referred to the father not as a dad but as a 'patriarch'. His comments to the newspaper were framed in such a way that you could imagine him kissing a gold signet ring on his pinkie or asking someone for a favour on their daughter's wedding day. Alongside the article were photos of the boys and patriarchs and consiglieri who were kicked off the cruise ship. The men wore colourful Hawaiian shirts stretched over their stomachs with braces to hold up their sagging pants. The boys wore grey tracksuits and singlets that covered their sloppy rigs. All looked more Australian than the fashionable, tight-bodied men of Rome and Milan.

Bankstown with its luxe Jeeps and Louis Vuitton bag aspirations. The property prices and the buildings keep rising to the sky. It's becoming more its own place.

The place has changed and so have its citizens. And the thing about these people who move through the place, metaphorically, spiritually and culturally, is that their identities morph like water itself. Their identities change shape based on the environment around them or the obstacles in their way.

Kamilla was someone who had changed her identity. It helped her land a partner, an apartment and a somewhat secure future, though it came at a cost. Regardless, trauma is a legitimate exchange for an exceptional life. When I changed my identity for Kane, I thought it might secure my place with him, bring us closer together. But I was just a tool, a device, one of the many people he used to get what he wanted.

In the suburb of Bankstown where Anglos become wogs and everyone wants the luxe car and latest LV, I realised that I had to change my actions, ways and beliefs to get what I wanted. And it was going to be uglier than caking my face with inch-thick foundation and as painful as a full body wax.

32.

I rented a car to take Mum on a daytrip to the seaside. My thinking was that long highways and seeing a place from her past might jolt her out of her obsessions. Perhaps when the salt air blasted her face, or the sand occupied her shoes, she might recall happy memories, I might see that ear-to-ear smile or hear that rosy-cheeked laugh. And I thought that after the trip she might agree to go into treatment, that there might be a change in her. Then I could have the cheesy Greek mother stereotype I always wanted.

The coastal suburb of Kurnell, southeast of Bankstown, was a place I had often heard old Greeks talking about. Every Australia Day, all the Sydney Greeks had a picnic at the place where Captain Cook first came ashore on Australian soil.

The tradition had died down now but in the past the whole area became a sea of picnic rugs and eskies filled with ouzo bottles. Once my mum had described going there herself; her eyes darted around, and she shook her hands in excitement when she told me about catching a tiny crab. A smile cracked her face. I stored that information in the back of my head.

Before I picked Mum up for the drive, I took the rented car to the Budget Auto Wash (cabin clean only) and they vacuumed the upholstery and wiped down the surfaces. It was a rainy day when I drove to the new Department of Housing place that I had helped get by becoming Me Mum. The sky threw a diffused light over my mum as she emerged from the one-bedroom house. Mum wore a crimson puffer jacket over a pink hoodie. She did her getting-into-the-car ritual. The car was clean, extra clean, but Mum still got into the car like it was a form of theatre.

Like theatre, it was part contrived performance, part pain and all exposition. She swung the passenger-side door open and put her head into the car. Eyes scanned for bits of dirt, and with one of her palms she would dust off the upholstery. Then she grasped the handle and swung her body into the seat. Her body rustled and settled, then she adjusted the headrest up and down.

I sighed as she continued to examine the seat and dust it off. While I drove she adjusted the air-con knobs and played with the buttons on the radio. She asked where we were going, and I told her it was a surprise. I took the highways and drove over a bridge. At the entrance to the national park I paid the booth attendant the toll. As we drove through the trees, Mum said that she hoped the men wouldn't see her going there. I ignored her and continued down Captain Cook Drive. There was scrub on one side and parklands on the other. She kept looking around, turning her head to stare at a particular tree or a dip in the embankment, then asking if I'd seen that.

As soon as I parked she escaped the car and pulled the pink hoodie over her head. Strands of grey hair straggled out the sides. She looked around at the hills and smiled, then pointed past the trees beyond us and said, That way. I locked the car and she ran towards the picnic area. I followed her, asking her to slow down. She walked past a statue of Captain Cook and asked him what he was looking at. The air felt chalky, cold. She ran up and over the slanted hills of the picnic area, her hair blowing everywhere. I crested the hill and saw her crouching where the rocks met the sea. A cute red ball of different materials. She picked up rocks quickly and brown crabs came running out from under them. Her hands reached for them, but they were too quick. She overreached and fell over.

A tiny sprinkle started to fall. I found a high rock to perch on, about twenty metres from her. She climbed around the rocks, finding new crevices to explore. Her body was old but tough. Her hand would grip a ledge as she lowered herself to the other side. A tiny wave would hit a rock, the afro would rise, and the wind would carry the spray towards me. My vision became blurry, but I was still aware of the fuzzy shape of my mother as she scuttled around the edges of the water, looking for crabs and asking the sea for answers. The drizzle was cold, and I pulled the hood of my rain shell over my head and zipped it up until it covered my mouth. I was two eyes in a black synthetic cover.

The rain became heavier. When it was beating down, I stood up and called out to her. Mum! I yelled. Mum! But my voice was lost among the crashing water and she was oblivious to the elements. She kept on upturning objects, old cans of fizzy drink, empty beer bottles. I climbed down from the rock and walked towards her. My shoes sank into the wet sand. She was crouching on the ground, fiddling with something in her hands. I reached out to put my hand on her shoulder.

She turned around to look up at me. The water fell continuously on her face. The crow's feet around her eyes filled with rainwater, becoming little creeks. Wrinkles in her forehead became rivers. The marionette lines under her mouth were waterfalls. Her nose was a precipice that took the brunt of the rain. Her eyes glowed as she looked up at me. She said she wanted to stay, this was a safe place, away from the men that were watching her.

Everything froze as I thought about leaving her. It would be easy to tell her that if she stayed there, among the sand and rocks and frothing water, the men wouldn't be able to follow her anymore. She would become an apparition in this place. Another ghost among the dead settlers. She would set up camp in the bush and become a tree lady. Shopping trolleys to store her things, a tarp tied around a trunk to make a shelter. She would be out of my life. No more random phone calls. No more paying her bills. No more her.

She asked, Do the men want us to go now?

I said, The rain wants us to go now.

She extended her hand to me and we put our slippery palms together. I pulled her up and we walked back to the car with my arm around her shoulder.

In the car I turned the air-con to warm. The rain shell hadn't protected me from the rain, and my shirt stuck to my body. I slowly turned up the knob, and heat blasted through the vents. Outside, the windscreen wipers had trouble clearing the glass.

As soon as we were back on the highway I pulled into a 7-Eleven. I left Mum in the car and went inside to get her a pre-mixed hot chocolate. As I peeled the foil from the cup and put it under the hot water dispenser, I looked out the window and saw my mother in the car. A taxi pulled up to a petrol pump. Hot water poured into the cup and I stirred the chocolate mixture. My gaze switched between the rental car and the taxi, worried that she would do the bolt.

When I brought the hot chocolate to her in the car, she wrapped both of her hands around the cup and lifted it to her mouth. She drank it slowly without lowering the cup, only her eyes visible over the rim. Before I drove her back to the one-bedder in Carramar, I said that I'd take her for a tour around the old neighbourhood.

As we got closer to the old apartment she had rented, the cup fell out of her hands; she pointed to a house as we drove by it. Her whole body started to shake in the seat and I pulled over to the kerb.

The house had a familiar balustrade and a concrete front yard. She had seen that house numerous times. She had done the bolt in front of it or stood there shaking or crying in front of it. Mum told the story through heaving breath.

She told me that a woman was murdered by her husband in that house. Mum remembered the woman clearly, because she had thick curly hair, and a husband with a good job. She also remembered that there was a young son, and that she envied the woman, and was worried that she had cursed her, in the way that Greeks believe they can curse someone through envy. Then one day there were two police cars in the driveway and one on the kerb out front. Uniforms stood on the concrete front yard and everything was silent. She saw the son coming out of the house, escorted by police, his head covered in a sheet.

I asked what happened to the father, to the son.

Mum said the father got limited time, because they found a knife in her hand.

And the son?

33.

I was walking with Basil from the cafe towards his car when an old woman flagged him down to say hello. I stood back to let them talk.

The woman was probably in her early seventies, with creaseless Mediterranean skin. A tiny gold cross hung around her neck. Her pants were black, her long-sleeved blouse had a spiral polka-dot frill, and she dragged a floral-patterned shopping trolley with two wheels.

They started talking and Basil dominated the conversation, asking how her new place was going, if her children had visited. She got in answers, but they were mainly one syllable. Basil was trying to wrap up the conversation, but the woman just stood there, blinking at him. She reached out to take his arm to anchor him to her. He promised he would visit her at the retirement village.

It was out of a protocol to my Greek elders, that I introduced myself to the woman and said I was writing a book about Basil. She repeated my name with a question at the end. Pano? When I confirmed it, her eyes swooped in on me. A single finger pushed an imaginary strand of hair behind her head. Come forward, child, she said and grabbed me by the arm. Her fingernails dug into my bicep as she dragged me away from Basil. I looked back at Basil standing up straight, hands clasped in front of him. A serious man standing in the wings of the church.

She told me her name was Asimo. It was an old-fashioned Greek name like my mum's, Froso. She curled her finger at me, indicating I should come closer, and put her palm alongside her mouth, telling me a secret. Basil was such a lovely man, she said. He had helped her sell her house when they found that parts of it were filled with asbestos. I looked over at Basil. He stood there with his hands clasped above his hips, watching us talk. She asked what I did, and I told her again that I was writing a book about Basil. And then she asked me my name again.

Elderly Greek women traditionally face two potential fates: either they become the matriarchal centre of their family and community or they just get hung out to dry.

The ones who become the mainstay of the Greek community have a soft, accepting way about them but still love to get a bit judgy-wudgy.

As the centre of the modern diasporic family, such a woman offers feudal remedies for all and sundry conditions. To treat a grandchild with the flu she might pull out the cotton balls, lighter and glass cups for good ancient Greek-style cupping, called vendouzes. If someone says a grandchild looks nice in her dress, she sews garlic under the hem. With her superstitions and love of pagan pseudo-medicine there is nothing she will not try to treat.

At family gatherings where her horde of Greeks conglomerate, her bung hip will be no obstacle. She will serve, making sure everyone has eaten. She will drink as much beer and ouzo as the men. She will separate fighting grandchildren and chastise her own children for being bad parents.

There are also elderly Greek women who are alienated, alone and betrayed. Their adult children have moved closer to the converted warehouse that house Fabian Strategies Public Relations where they work and are too busy feng shui-ing all the negativity out of their newly furnished loft apartment. The Eames chair does not go next to a mirror! It's bad yin energy!

This move away from the mother was deliberate. An old wog decked out in Dannii Minogue Petites for Target does not accessorise well with a young woman holding a Bao Bao Issey Miyake Lucent tote. The son or daughter sets their mum up in a place in the old neighbourhood and then never contacts her again.

The lonely, hung-out-to-dry Greek matriarch takes her seething undercurrent of anger out on pokie machines or her regular taxi driver. She wanders the streets.

It's easy to identify which type of Greek matriarch one encounters in the street. And Asimo, seemed to want too much conversation, indicating that her children didn't call her much. Basil interrupted the conversation, pulling my arm. Nice seeing you, he kept repeating to Asimo, stepping away slowly. Nice seeing you.

This situation wasn't unusual. Wherever we went, Basil knew someone. He was an in-the-round theatre event the audience watched agog but never remembered – there was too much spectacle to recall the actual content. In Basil's case, the spectacle was the shiny poly blends, skin-tight button-down shirts and shark-clean teeth. Bodies can have a charisma and the things that decorate them can be just as alluring.

As we walked away from Asimo, there was a silence between us. I filled it by telling Basil about my mum. Told him about growing up with her. About the trip to the community health clinic and the failed interventions. And about how I gave up trying to change her and moved her into public housing. Basil's face was completely blank, I offered him personal information that he could benefit from and he wasn't going to offer any information back.

He bowed his head as we walked, scrunching up his face. Uh-huh, uh-huh. The only thing he asked was where she lived now. I told him that it was on a block in Carramar. Basil stopped and turned to me. Ya know that place is onna river, prime fucking land for a developer, if they got their hands onnit.

Basil only showed me things that he wanted me to see. So when I saw his calendar, it was access to a part of him he wouldn't display. That's why I took the photo. Click. I had this need to find out more and to do this, I tapped into a part of myself that I thought I was done with. The part of me that looked through people's windows and watched them in the dark. This desire strengthened the pillar inside me and filled my mouth with saliva.

34.

A few days after seeing Basil I rented a mid-noughties white Toyota Camry. When I picked it up from the hire office, I saw the bonnet had faded from sun exposure and there were dents in the side. It looked like a car for drug dealers going incognito or Asian families taking their kids to tutoring.

Keating's Storage World was in the industrial part of Bankstown. I wondered if it was named after the prime minister and pig farm owner who came from the area. Paul Keating was our most Australian prime minister. He had swarthy Black Irish looks and had married a flight attendant, the ultimate working-class mile-high dream. He called his enemy 'a low-altitude flyer' and 'a 24-carat pissant'. He differentiated himself from the victims of his acerbic language by wearing precision-cut Zegna suits. Keating's high-flying ways represented a broader shift in the aspirations of the traditional Aussie battler. The workers' paradise of the past was gone: now the Aussie battler wanted a few investment homes, well-made suits and jet-setting holidays. Those ideas must have ambushed me growing up in the 1980s, snuck into my mind in a coup de main.

The dollar sign mountain was something I wasn't climbing; I was living in a shitty rental and had an at-risk bank account. I thought about how I could get ahead and realised that I had my own resources that I could mine. Parts of my past, parts of my background that I could use. So I too could fly at a high altitude.

I pulled up outside Keating's Storage World half an hour before Basil was due to be there. A sign with bright-orange lettering that read KEATING'S hung across the chain-link fence at the front. Next to the entry was a small reception office, the garages sprawling behind it. The place was so big, cars stopped at the office, looked at a map and then drove to their storage garage.

While I sucked on my coffee and waited, I took in my surrounds. Around me were warehouses and grim-looking offices. It was the kind of place where data entry temps came and flirted with forklift drivers. The industrial park was off a main arterial, and at night sex workers strutted down the road pretending it was a catwalk. Sternly worded signs had

been erected around the buildings – THIS AREA IS BEING
CONSTANTLY MONITORED and ANTISOCIAL ACTIVITIES
WILL NOT BE TOLERATED. But in this bastion of business
mediocrity there would no doubt have been a few disgraced
copywriters with constantly sniffing noses who had groped an
intern's buttocks. What they really meant was COULD THE
POOR STOP HAVING DRUGS AND SEX?

I waited in the car with the radio off so I could pay attention to what was going on outside. Cars, trucks and utes drove
in and out of Keating's Storage World. A young woman in a
hatchback with frangipani-shaped stickers on the windscreen
pulled up at the front office and went inside. She came out
juggling a stack of flat-pack moving boxes, jammed them into
the boot and drove off. A big truck with a storage container
on the back stopped in the driveway, blocking the entry.
Its driver, a short man in a blue singlet, jumped out of the
cabin and went into the reception office without bothering
to look around. A car behind the truck waited a minute and
then beeped its horn a few times until the truck driver came
running out. He put up his hand apologetically, jumped back
into the cabin and took off into the storage world.

I was staring at an elegant gum tree when a flatbed turned
into the driveway. UTE RENTALS was emblazoned across the
driver's door. I saw the back of a head that I recognised. It was
shaved with a fresh cut and the hair on top was brown and
slicked down. Through the back window of the ute's cabin I

saw that the man was wearing a shiny black T-shirt. The ute disappeared into the lanes of the storage world. I looked at the clock on the dashboard. He was right on time.

I turned the key in the ignition, and the engine revved. I pulled into the driveway, passed the front office and followed the signs that said LARGE-SCALE STORAGE. My windshield became a screen filled with rows and rows of garages.

The small driveway gave no indication of the grandeur and size of the place. It was almost as big as a housing estate. I wondered how many failed dreams were locked down here, unvisited. Staying in second gear, I turned down the first row of garages. Between each orange garage door was a white stucco wall. Orange. White. Orange. White. When I got to the end I realised I would have to drive up and down the lanes to find Basil's ute.

But as soon as I turned into the next row I saw the rental ute parked next to an open garage. It was at least two hundred metres away. I quickly put the car into reverse and backed around the corner. I pulled over beside a wall and got out of the car. First I peeked around the corner, then I took a longer look.

Basil wore aviator sunglasses, a white dust mask over his mouth and small shorts exposing glistening man thigh. From this distance I couldn't tell if his legs were shining from a fresh wax or a spray tan. He was going in and out of the garage, bringing out black-plastic-covered blocks that he loaded into the back of the ute. The blocks were almost two metres long, but he carried them easily, as though they were light. Then, as he was putting one block into the back of the ute, he lost his grip and dropped it on the ground. The black plastic came open and out fell a grey fibrous block, flakes of it falling away. Basil took off his shirt and wrapped it around the bottom of his face, over the mask. His bare torso was brown and hairless with overdeveloped pec muscles. He rewrapped the block in the plastic and threw it into the ute. Then he got a blue tarp from the back and covered the tray.

I kept looking at his hairless legs. I could see the bulbous thigh meeting the knee and the ripples in his calf muscles. Their shine and shape must have put me in a trance because I didn't notice that he had started to walk towards me. He must have seen my weird head sticking out past the edge of the wall. His arms were swinging by his sides, and the bottom part of his face was still covered by the black wicking material of his shirt.

35.

What the fuck are you doing here? Basil's voice was muffled by the shirt around his face. He strode towards me, his body was plank-stiff and the veins popped in his arms. With one hand he unwrapped the shirt from around his face and tore off the dust mask. He snatched off his sunglasses and threw them against the wall.

His high-end sports shoes walked towards me, his torso inflated, and my torso shrank. I raised my hands, palms out, trying to make him calm down. He only increased his speed. I shook my hands, said, Wait, wait, wait, and he shot out his arms and grabbed my collar in his fists. We were chin to chin. From between his teeth he asked again what the fuck I was doing there. A sprinkle of spit landed on my lips. I could feel the moisture of his breath pouring into my mouth.

His arms tugged me forwards and he headbutted me. Our heads crashed, a hollow sound. The pain splintered across my forehead and I panted, too shocked to answer him. He pushed me against the stucco wall, little spikes going into my back. My T-shirt ripped around my neck as he grabbed me again, screaming, pushing his torso into me, chest to chest. My nostrils filled with his scent, my body immobilised with fear.

His nose touched my nose as he yelled at me. Hands on my crew-neck, tearing it apart, his pecs against me felt like stone. His body at the mercy of a hot rage that he couldn't understand himself. There was something broken in that man and it couldn't be fixed.

To change the energy, I jutted my head forwards so our lips were touching and stuck out my tongue. Basil's face froze. I licked from his bottom lip, over his top lip to the bottom of his nose. I tasted the salt of his skin. He stepped backwards, stumbled and fell back onto the concrete. He used the back of his hand to wipe his mouth. He looked up at me, his eyes big holes, his mouth contorting with anger.

I held my hand out and told him to calm down, that I would ride with him in his ute and tell him everything I knew. He sat there for a minute and looked around the storage space. All the other garages were closed. There was no one else around. We both knew he could easily kill me if he decided to.

Basil got up and wiped his palms on his shorts. As I went to pick up his shirt I walked past his mangled sunglasses. The lenses had cracked in the frames and the golden black arms were bent. I said to him that he might need some new Versace sunglasses. Basil looked at me in disgust, but I could tell he was really disgusted that my tongue slobbered over his mouth. Don't worry, I said, if you hear my plan you'll have more Versace than the Illuminati.

We walked to the ute in silence. Basil closed and locked the garage door and I helped him finish covering the tray of the ute with the tarp.

As we were securing the corners, I told him the address we were going to, and he looked at me, confused. His lips pursed, ready to argue. I took a few steps back and told him that I had looked at his schedule when I was interviewing Kamilla. I left the information hanging there and got into the passenger seat of the ute. Fucking Kamilla, he hissed. I realised that when he got home Kamilla was going to get it but I didn't care.

As I pulled my seatbelt across, Basil got into the cabin. He put the key in the ignition and started the engine – then he turned it back off and threw the keys out the window.

We're fuckin not goin anywhere till ya tell me what ya know and what ya want.

I wound the window handle, it was old and the glass squeaked rhythmically as the pane lowered. The air came into the cabin and settled in between the armrests and the confession. I found a packet of Dunhill's on the dashboard and lit one up.

⊞

It was the old Greek women in the street, Asimo. Such an old-fashioned Greek name, and there was something very familiar about her and the tiny gold cross around her neck. She reminded me of the many Greek women I had met during my childhood.

Asimo particularly reminded me of a woman called Thoula. One day Thoula stood on our balcony surrounded by pot plants filled to the brim with cigarette butts and tried to convince my mum to go to hospital. And then Mum said something to permanently end their friendship. Well, you would know about hospitals; your husband has fucked so many nurses! Thoula threw her cigarette case into her handbag and left. Mum said she was being honest.

I remembered how Asimo stood on the footpath holding her shopping trolley behind her and looked directly at Basil, whereas Basil looked up and away as he spoke to her. I saw that familiar trope from Southern European communities, where the women speak to men while looking at them and the men won't hold their gaze. It represented the power that women give to men, even if the men haven't earned it. I remembered what she said too: that Basil had helped her move out of her home when someone discovered asbestos there.

After meeting Asimo I went home and googled her. One of the first hits for the keywords 'Asimo' and 'asbestos' was from the local newspaper. I clicked on the article and there was a picture of Asimo leaning against her brick fence in front of a bungalow that had been modified with Greek pillars and statues of lions. Her arms were open, her palms facing the sky, a gesture that was part question and part despair. The headline was 'Grandmother's Asbestos Shocker'. The caption read: 'Asimo says she didn't realise she was living in an asbestos-filled house until it was mentioned to her by a passing stranger; now she doesn't know what to do!'

It only took a tiny amount of legwork to find out her address. The article mentioned that one of her favourite things to do was feed the ducks in the park opposite her house– there was only one park with a lake and ducks in Bankstown area. So I went to Maluga Passive Park and walked around it. I looked on the street to see if I could find any hints to her old house.

I found a house with columns out the front, concrete front yard and knocked on the door. Two old Greeks opened the door and in my fanciest and most respectful Greek I asked the old wogs inside the house if they knew Asimo. They pointed to where her house used to be, where some new duplexes had been built.

And when I found Asimo's address, it wasn't hard to check the internet sales history of her house. I found out that it was purchased cheaply by Vas Bros Real Estate and then sold two years later, after it had been redeveloped into townhouses.

Some googling, some local knowledge, a coffee with some old wogs, a property sales history search and I had it all clocked.

⊞

Basil's head was bowed, his arms bent, hands holding the steering wheel at the top.

The cigarette smoke created circles around my head. I told Basil it was a safe bet there was no asbestos in Asimo's house until he put it there. He asked if I was going to write about this. I lied to him and told him that I had already prepared an article for insurance purposes. If anything happened to me, it would be emailed to the right editors. His arms dangled and his breathing became quicker and deeper. He looked out the window to the splendid vision of orange garage doors. Nice view, I said to him, but if you come with me, I reckon I could get you a bigger payday, although I'll need a cut. I told him that we would need the asbestos blocks in the back of the ute.

We drove out of the industrial area and through Bankstown. Factory and business parks became highways. Kebab shops and

Awafi-slash-car washes turned into houses and apartment blocks. We drove up Henry Lawson Drive, on one side of us was the river. There were groups of fishermen on the river-bank. Fathers and sons, mates from the local soccer team. All were sitting on fold-out chairs, holding beers and rods. Brightly coloured buckets sat next to them in anticipation of the catch.

As I was telling the Asimo story to Basil, my palm connected to the dash just above the glove box – *thwack* – it happened repeatedly as I emphasised each point. I didn't know that I could be this kind of person. The monologue filled up the cabin around us, there was no place for Basil to go. I realised was controlling the space. Away from where he could see, I ran my knuckles against the leather seat that I was sitting on. Up and down the leather seat on my side. I could feel the smooth black skin on my fingers and I pretended it was Basil's body.

Powered up from his weakness, I told Basil that I could feel the prose poems that I had been trying to write coming back.

I wasn't worried about Basil anymore. He sat next to me, upright, smoking darts quickly, with one hand on the wheel as he drove. His chest was gleaming with sweat. We turned onto the highway and got into the left lane. Cars sped past us and I told him he was driving too slowly. Don't be nervous, I said. My eyes focused on landmarks around us so I could direct Basil to our destination. I told him to put out the cigarette and speed up. His legs didn't look as big as when I first saw them and nothing in me stirred. No arousal. No desire.

As we drove down the Henry Lawson historic route, brown signs informed us of the area's contribution to Australian literature. I explained its heritage to Basil, I think his house was here, I waved in a direction, hoping to distract him from the task at hand.

We went through an intersection where the highways met. Every time we passed a crane I pointed it out to Basil. There were cranes in empty lots, cranes on half-built buildings, cranes being transported on trucks. I told him that in the future months he would require one.

I pointed the way down the highway and told Basil that my mum lived in government housing next to the river. You remember, eh? You said it was prime real estate. He asked what we were going to do there. I told him we were going to put asbestos in her ceiling, without her knowledge. His chin went into his neck and he squinted. After he put the asbestos there, he would spend tomorrow making phone calls. Government departments would quickly realise that it was easier to sell the complex than do a clean-up. Privatisation was the way of the future.

Basil asked a volley of questions. What will happen to your mum when I buy the place? You gonna let her go homeless? How will you hide it from your mum?

Don't worry about her, I said to him. His concern confused me. Here was a man who bashed his girlfriend. In high school he fucked everything in sight with no care or consequence. And suddenly he cared about the plight of women. I told Basil that she needed to learn to take care of herself now. I said the kind of shit that capitalists love hearing – it's a dog-eat-dog world – and Basil nodded. I said to him, God doesn't give you anything you can't handle – that was how I saw this situation for my mum. Basil went hmm and seriously thought about what I said.

We turned off the highway into the suburb where my mum lived. What I saw around me reminded me how the people without dreams lived. There were apartment blocks closer to the train station. Carramar had pretty areas where the old wogs lived – you could see the well-maintained Italian and Greek houses with thirty-year-old olive and lemon trees in their front yards. The shopping strip was full of people pushing trolleys. All the shops had security bars over their windows. I'd better be getting a good finder's fee, I said to Basil.

I looked out the car window.

My money dreams included a finder's fee that would be enough for a down payment on a studio apartment close to the city. Inside there would be a simple, grey modular sofa and an elegant bed. Trade could drop by for a quickie. I would have a lube dispenser attached to the wall. In the money dream,

I was already lying front down, my back stinging at the medical laser that was being used to permanently remove the hair off my body. With my hairless back, I would do the Bondi walk, and meet gay associates for brunch, all of us with studio apartments and hair-free backs. There would be overseas holidays too – Mykonos for Xlsior. Bali for Mardi Gras recovery. I was already on the travellator in the airport, neck pillow in tow.

36.

The ute's bullbar pulled up to a chain-link fence, beyond it were semi-detached one-bedroom houses, all lined up next to each other, their front doors, stairs and windows all in the same place. Discarded couches and broken appliances lay on the grass in front of the complex. Letterboxes spewed uncollected mail and catalogues. Each house had a few small steps leading to a front door. I remembered immediately which house was my mum's. Even if I hadn't, I would have easily identified her place from the foil that covered the inside of the windows and the decorations on the front door. A group of marble blue eyes hung on chains. There were so many that it looked as though the door was mutating into a face with multiple eyes.

I knocked on the door, three solid raps. As I waited I turned to look at Basil standing next to the ute. From inside I heard Mum shuffle to the door. As she opened it, the hinges gave a long, slow creak and the amulet-baubles tinkled against each other. Her eyes expanded as she opened the door, the eyelids formed full circles, the black colour seemed more solid than I remembered. She stood there in an oversized red T-shirt that went down to her calves. Her legs held the ground down and wrinkles drew contempt on her face. Her grey hair had been chopped off, it was in tufts around her head and her fringe was still cut on a slant. A loud click came out of her mouth. Panagiotaki . . . you finally remember you have a mother, she said. I shook my head at her. I wanted to tell her that she had failed at being a mother. Instead I stood back and pointed to Basil and told her that I had brought someone with me.

Her eyes ran up and down Basil and she commented on how handsome he was. I ignored this and walked past her into the one-bedroom house. The living area contained a small kitchenette and a couch. There were piles of newspapers everywhere. Letters were stacked on the couch, and multiple jars of Nad's hair removal goo were all over the kitchen counter.

Mum invited Basil into the house. She asked him if he wanted a glass of water, and went to get an old jar and wash it. As she turned on the tap I told her to stop. I told her Basil's full name. Her mouth pursed, she looked at me and turned around to examine him again. He stood frozen at the front door.

The tap was still on. Water flowed into the kitchen sink. Fingers of light came in around the edges of the foil-covered window. One of Mum's eyes crinkled, and her hands started to shake in shock. She reached out her arms towards him, trying to touch his aura. Her eyes blinked rapidly. Her language broke down, and she let out words in little bits. She said that she remembered his house, the one with the pillars.

Basil stood just beyond the frame of the front door. He became a cheap concrete statue like the ones in the front yard of a wog's house.

I stepped between my mum and Basil and extended my arms, just in case she launched at him. Mum said she had never met Basil but she knew his father. She pointed her finger and pressed the air to emphasise a point. Spiro, the man who was a builder of homes and a killer of his wife. All the community talked about him, she said. Basil looked at me and I knew it was true. He held on to the doorframe and the colour ran from his face. My head involuntarily nodded. At that moment I knew what had happened to Basil's mother.

Basil was still frozen at the door, his head bowed and his face emotionless. My mum rubbed her hands through her hair. I looked at Basil's profile: he had his father's nose but the high cheekbones of his mother. A little boy came out of a house, his hand held by police, his head covered by a sheet.

Our three bodies seemed like debris in the house. The walls were painted in a sick pink, and there were some water marks in the corners that made it seem like the fibro was crying.

I told Basil that I was going to take my mum out so he could do what he needed to do in the roof. When I turned to my mum, she was still crying and shaking. She was hunched over the sink. The tap was running water and I reached out to hold her hand.

ACKNOWLEDGEMENTS

This book initially was workshopped in SWEATSHOP. Thank you to all those in the collective who gave feedback and especially to:

Mohammed Ahmad

Winnie Dunn

Stephen Pham

Maryam Azam

Shirley Lee

Omar Sakr

Everyone at Hachette. Especially Robert Watkins and Brigid Mullane who even in this book's ruins saw potential. I'm so grateful to have both of you working on this.

Thanks also to:
- Clara Finlay
- Dženana Vucic
- Jenny Topham
- Lydia Tasker
- Sarah Holmes
- Fiona Hazard
- Louise Sherwin-Stark

All praise and worship to my oracles and muses:
- Rosie Dennis
- Lina Kastoumis
- Yasmin Hunter
- Seide Ramadani
- Christina Ra

Thanks to my family:
- James Carleton
- Avraam, Leonidas and Petros
- Anastasia Polites
- Mina Polites
- Patrick Heeger

Peter Polites is a writer of Greek descent from Western Sydney. As part of the SWEATSHOP writers collective, Peter has written and performed pieces all over Australia.

His first novel, *Down the Hume*, was shortlisted for a NSW Premier's Literary Award in 2017. *The Pillars* is his second novel.

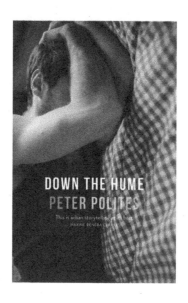

SHORTLISTED FOR NSW PREMIER'S LITERARY AWARDS MULTICULTURAL NSW AWARD 2018

A novel of addiction, secrets and misplaced love, this is an Australian debut not to be missed.

How did Bucky get here? A series of accidents. A tragic love for a violent man. An addiction to painkillers he can't seem to kick. An unlikely friendship with an ageing patient.

Drugs, memories and the objects of his desire are colluding against Bucky. And when it hits him. Bam. A ton of bricks . . .

The shadowy places of Western Sydney can be lit up with the hope of love, but no streetlight can illuminate like obsession.